RICH WIDOWS OF SAVANNAH VALLEY

YOU'VE EARNED IT, LADIES

MITZI PERDUE

RICH WIDOWS OF SAVANNAH VALLEY:
YOU'VE EARNED IT, LADIES

Quantity sales special discounts are available on quantity purchases by corporations, associations, and others. For details, contact the publisher at carol@markvictorhansenlibrary.com

Orders by U.S. trade bookstores and wholesalers.
Email: carol@markvictorhansenlibrary.com

Creative contribution by Amy Keane and Carol McManus.
Cover Design - Low & Joe Creative, Brea, CA 92821
Illustrations - Bob Eckstein
Book Layout - DBree, StoneBear Design

Manufactured and printed in the United States of America distributed globally by markvictorhansenlibrary.com

New York | Los Angeles | London | Sydney

ISBN: 979-8-88581-000-5 Hardback
ISBN: 979-8-88581-001-2 Paperback
ISBN: 979-8-88581-002-9 eBook
Library of Congress Control Number: 2022901973

THE SAVANNAH VALLEY SERIES

Everyone imagines what life will be like in retirement. Perhaps you know someone who ended up in a depressing nursing facility with people who didn't care about their health and wellbeing. That's not the way it has to be and that's not the way it is in Savannah Valley.

The characters in these books celebrate life and retirement in fun and imaginative ways after facing unexpected challenges. Here, new friendships are made, new horizons open, and a lifetime of experience and acquired wealth is celebrated.

Each book in the series is inspired by true events unique to each author. Sit back, relax, and allow yourself to be transported to the glorious and prestigious retirement community known as Savannah Valley.

Rich Widows of Savannah Valley
by Mitzi Perdue

All About Henry : Rich Widower of Savannah Valley
by Lyle Lee Jenkins

Love After : Dreams Still Come True
by Russell Gray & Mona Guarino

Maestro : Songteller of Savannah Valley
by Rick & Stacie Fessler

Nightingale : Say Goodbye to Yesterday
by Tony Lopes

Ruby : Magic Comes From the Heart
by Randall Kenneth Jones

markvictorhansenlibrary.com/savannah-valley

CONTENTS

PROLOGUE

Welcome to an adventure!

I've noticed something as a Sheraton Heiress. (My late father co-founded and was President of the Sheraton Hotel Chain, although the family sold it at the time of his death.) People are curious about what the lives of people are like who ...what's a nice way of putting this? One that won't turn you off, because honest, I want you to join me for a fun adventure with the Rich Widows, and I want you to find this story relatable!

OK, I'll try that sentence again. I've noticed that when I get to know someone well, they often want to know what my life is like. What's it like to be able to afford the finest of everything and go first class every time? What's high society like? What's it like to go to amazing parties and wear designer clothes?

I know what that life is like, and truthfully, it's been an amazing journey, meeting fabulous people, traveling to exciting places, and squeezing a lot of scrumptious moments into each day! I want you to get lost in this reading journey with me and have a little fun of your own as you get to experience that life vicariously, diving into the adventures of four very rich widows.

This book is based on people I've known and lifestyles that I've witnessed. The lifestyles are real, although in the interest of full disclosure, my family and career success has always been more important than spending money. I wanted to play full out in the big leagues of success with the big boys!

My career has been writing and media. For a good bit of my adult life, I wrote a column for *Scripps Howard* called, "The Environment and You", and today I write about Human Trafficking for *Psychology Today* and for the *Association of Foreign Press Correspondents*, as well as doing TV and radio.

So why did I write *Rich Widows*?

I wrote it for you! As a lifelong writer and lover of life, I felt there was a big need for people who are classified as seniors, who are still vital, having fun, and feeling young. We needed our own stories of romance, friendship, and adventure. I couldn't find them, so I decided to write one! If you're like me and you feel all the wisdom, experience, and savvy you've gained through the years gives you that extra zest for life then buckle up. What you're about to read is an Adventure for Seniors!

Enjoy! Have fun! Get ready to meet Glenda, and her soon-to-be best friends, the *Rich Widows of Savannah Valley*.

Love,
Mitzi Perdue (Mrs. Frank Perdue)

CHAPTER ONE

Arrivals

Glenda slowed from a full-on run to a brisk jog as she approached 32 Peach Street. Residents began to arrive at Savannah Valley two weeks prior, but rumors regarding the status of this particular property had spread like wildfire throughout the community. Its owner had passed on sixteen days before his move-in date, and the scuttlebutt was that despite Savannah Valley's 55-plus age requirement, his thirty-something mistress would occupy it in his stead. She was spotted removing boxes from her strange vehicle and carrying them into the house by herself.

Sure enough, there it sat in the driveway, a shiny silver thing that resembled one of those cars from *Back to the Future*. But bigger, like an SUV, crossed with a spaceship. And there she was as well, a woman holding a large cardboard box, wearing cutoff jean shorts and a black T-shirt, her brown curly hair pulled back in a ponytail. Glenda paused by the mailbox, jogging in place as she pondered whether she should say hello and attempt to get the story straight from the horse's mouth or mind her own darn business and finish her run. She was still mulling it over when the woman called out to her.

"Hi, I'm Sharon Wright. Yes, I'm old enough to live here. No, I'm not anyone's mistress. I'm leasing the property from the estate holders. That's it—that's the story. Have a great day."

Glenda, feeling just the tiniest bit guilty for giving credence to idle gossip, decided a proper introduction was now imperative. She jogged down the driveway toward Sharon, stopping to offer her right hand in greeting as soon as she was within arm's length.

"Well, hi yourself, Sharon Wright. I'm Glenda Edelman. Pleased to make your acquaintance."

Sharon looked Glenda up and down, noting her perfectly coordinated running gear, which included fuchsia shorts, baby pink tank top with fuchsia insets, baby pink sneakers, and a pink floral print baseball cap. She set her box down on the concrete driveway, wiped her hands on her shorts, then shook Glenda's hand.

"Nice to meet you, too, Glenda. Apologies for shouting at you. This is the tenth time today that someone gawked at me. Thankfully, Darcy from over on Moon River Court stopped by and filled me in on *why* they were gawking. I'm used to people thinking I'm younger than I am, but the 'mistress' bit—that's a sparkling new adventure."

Glenda grinned. "Trust me when I say that having folks think you appear younger than your years becomes ever more enjoyable with each passing birthday."

Sharon pointed at Glenda, smirking. "You do realize that this means it's time to play 'Guess My Age,' don't you?"

"Well, it'll be easy for me since you mentioned you're old enough to reside in Savannah Valley." Glenda squinted, tapping her index finger on her lips. "I'd say thirty-six, but given the circumstances, I'll say fifty-five since that's as low as we can go here."

Sharon nodded. "Spot on, Glenda. Fifty-five it is. Man, thirty-six seems like a week ago. I'm going with sixty-four for you."

Glenda put her hands on her hips, smiling. "I turned eighty this past March."

"Holy moly, that's insane. You look unbelievably fabulous."

Glenda laughed. "See what I mean?"

The hum of an electric golf cart approaching turned their attention to the road. As it pulled into the driveway, Sharon recognized the driver as Darcy Peterson, the woman who'd been kind enough to stop by earlier to let her know some of the other residents were talking trash about her. Sharon had yet to meet the woman in the passenger seat, but she was waving just as enthusiastically as Darcy. As soon as the cart came to a stop, they both hopped out, Darcy holding a large baking dish with a bright green ribbon tied around it.

“Sharon. Look, we baked chocolate chip and salted caramel brownies for you.” Darcy was wearing the same tie-dye apron over the short black tank dress she wore earlier when Sharon met her. A sporty lime-green headband tamed her wavy salt-and-pepper hair. Her companion, dressed in a tan miniskirt and white polo shirt, had black hair, the shiny straight kind all women envied. Darcy glanced her way, then back at Sharon. “Oh, whoopsie. Pardon my manners. Sharon, this is Edith Adams. She’s over on Trolley Drive.”

Edith stepped forward to shake Sharon’s hand. “I, too, have been the subject of the Savannah Valley gossip gaggle. They were calling me ‘Trolley Trollop’ because they heard I was married four times. But, since you arrived, that’s yesterday’s news. So, thanks for that.”

Sharon chuckled. “I would say you’re so not welcome, but you brought brownies, so it’s fine.” She turned and waved her hand in Glenda’s direction. “This is Glenda Edelman. I just learned that she’s eighty. Needless to say, that blows my mind, and I’m seriously considering taking up running—after eating all the brownies, of course.”

All the ladies laughed, and Glenda shook hands with Darcy and Edith in turn. “Lovely to meet you both. I suppose now you have to fess up to how many times you’ve gone ‘round the sun so we’ll all have some dirt on each other.”

Darcy pushed her red cat-eyed glasses back into place. "I am proud to say that despite all the abuse my body has tolerated—nay, endured—that number is seventy-two."

Edith put her hands on her hips. "Sixty-one for me. How about you, Sharon?"

"Fifty-five and feeling uncharacteristically generous. Who wants to come inside and see all the spectacular color schemes and furniture I had absolutely nothing to do with choosing? You can share those brownies with me."

***

The ladies snacked at the kitchen island, seated on backless, swiveling bar stools, which Sharon claimed would be the death of her one day. Edith poured red wine in the plastic cups she just happened to bring along for the ride. Though the home was leased as fully furnished, no dishes, glasses, utensils, or small kitchen appliances were included. Sharon finished the last bite of her third brownie and apologized once again for the lack of proper service items.

"Super sorry for not having the basics. I haven't stayed here overnight yet, and I've been eating at the Bohemian, the hotel I'm staying at for the time being. It's got a fantastic riverfront view, so I wasn't in a rush to get the kitchen set up."

Glenda patted Sharon's hand. "Honey, I am not above drinking wine straight from the bottle if the need arises."

Edith raised her plastic cup. "Cheers to that, Glenda."

They tapped their cups together. Darcy cleared her throat then spoke, as if blushing at the prospect of expressing her feelings and, perhaps, being rejected. "Well, ladies, this was unexpected, but an absolute delight. Perhaps we could all sit together at tonight's official welcome dinner? That way, there's a good chance we'll avoid getting stuck at a table with someone we don't know."

Glenda interrupted her. "Darcy, that is a most excellent suggestion. Yes, let's, please." Edith and Sharon nodded in agreement.

Darcy dazzled them with a broad grin. "Well, now I'm excited about something I was thoroughly dreading." She shook her head. "Isn't life so strange? Edith and I met this morning at the pool. But Sharon, Glenda, our paths may not have crossed if it wasn't for a nasty rumor. Not so soon, anyway. Perhaps the gossip gaggle is due a thank you."

Edith snorted. "If the thank you is leaving a flaming bag of dog poop on their doorsteps, I'm in."

They dissolved into laughter, sobering when Glenda commented that she'd never wanted a dog but would now be willing to consider purchasing several large ones—purely for protection, of course.

Ten minutes and one empty baking dish later, Sharon escorted them outside. Edith pointed at the vehicle in the driveway. "Tesla Cybertruck?"

Sharon's jaw dropped open in surprise. "Wow, yes. Yes, it is. You're familiar with the line?"

Edith grinned. "One of my ex-husbands had an original Tesla Roadster. He loved that car more than anything, including me. It's mine now, sitting in a storage unit back in Boston. Too fast for my taste, but I enjoy knowing he'll never see it again."

Sharon clapped her hands together three times, and Darcy and Glenda joined in. Sharon extended her palms to the sky and shrugged. "Well, mine does seat up to six people. Maybe I should pick everyone up so we can arrive at the welcome dinner together? Five-thirty?"

Three yeses rang out as one, and the women parted ways, so they'd have enough time to ready themselves for the evening. There was, after all, a specific dress code for all meals served at Savannah Valley, and they certainly wouldn't want to ruffle any feathers, would they?

CHAPTER TWO

Welcome to Savannah Valley

All eyes were on the women as they exited the Cybertruck, the valet's mouth dropping open as Sharon handed him the key fob. The welcome celebration dinner was black-tie only, and Glenda chose a purple single-shoulder silk evening dress for the occasion. Sharon opted for a black knee-length turtleneck sweater dress with circular cutouts on the sleeves; Darcy, a fringed multicolored sequined tea-length dress, and Edith a floor-length orange pleated gown with halter straps and a sweetheart neckline. Together, they strode up the red carpet rolled out in place for the evening and entered the Tower. The building sat on the highest point of Savannah Valley's property and featured nine restaurants, two each on the first four floors and one on the sixth, called Sky, where the welcome celebration was taking place.

The ladies, except for Sharon, had previously dined in at least one of the Tower's eateries, but none of them experienced Sky as it was strictly off-limits to residents until this evening. As they walked across the rosewood floors toward the bank of four stainless and glass elevators, Darcy pointed at Glenda. "Your dress. Is it a Halston?"

Glenda twirled in a circle. "Indeed, it is."

Darcy nodded. "Thought so. Who's the lender?"

"Lender?" Glenda chuckled. "My closet, I guess. I bought it when it was introduced back in the seventies. I saw it during a private collection showing and just had to have it."

The doors of the far-left elevator opened, and the ladies entered, quickly pressing the number six button, hoping the doors would close before anyone else joined them. The doors slid shut, and as the elevator rose, Sharon and Edith high-fived each other.

Darcy was speechless, shaking her head before finding her voice again. "I'm sorry. Did I just hear you say you were at one of Halston's private collection showings? I mean, he's—yowza. He's my favorite designer of all time." She pointed at her dress. "I borrowed this piece of his from the MET Museum, and the reason they let me do it is that I helped curate their Halston collection. It's a spare that's missing a lot of beadwork, and I still had to sign my life away. If you wouldn't mind, I'd love to talk about the show sometime. I never got to meet him in person."

"Darcy, it would be my pleasure. I didn't get out much during that time since my children were small, but we were at the same party once. Liza, too. There may or may not be a few photos tucked away somewhere in my albums." Glenda winked and smiled.

Darcy gasped and placed her hand over her heart.

"Oh. My. God. Bless you, Glenda. I can't wait to hear it all. And maybe see some of it as well." She turned to Sharon and Edith, studying their dresses. "Edith, yours has to be Dolce and Gabbana. And Sharon, hmm, Prada, I believe?"

Edith nodded, and Sharon shrugged. "Let's go with that. I liked the holes, and I figured it would look cool with my boots." She held up her left foot. "Patent Diva Darcies, aka my dress-up Doc Martens."

Laughing, Darcy bent down to inspect them. "If these come in bright colors, I'm buying a pair. I feel obligated since they bear my name."

With a ding, the elevator doors slid open, and as they stepped out onto the black granite floor, Edith let out a soft wolf whistle. "Sheesh, now I get why they called it Sky."

Floor-to-ceiling seamless windows on all four sides allowed for an unobstructed 360-degree view of Savannah Valley. A large outdoor area was visible across the dining room interior, providing an uninterrupted flow between the space made possible by folding glass doors. The ebony-wood tables were all four-tops, each with matching wood chairs and a white tablecloth. The hostess, clad in a black tuxedo dress, half bowed in greeting.

"Welcome to the Tower. My name is Jensen, and we're so glad you could join us this evening. Party of four?" Edith nodded, and Jensen smiled. "Please, follow me."

Jensen seated them in the last row at the far right

of the room. As they settled in and looked around, they noticed theirs was the only full table so far. There were a few couples, but primarily singletons.

Sharon gave Darcy a thumbs up. "Good call on us sitting together. If I'd been sitting alone and Jensen brought me a dinner pal, I would have excused myself and never returned."

Glenda was examining the centerpiece. "I've never seen an oak bonsai before. And look, that's Spanish moss around the bottom. Very on-brand for Savannah. Kudos to the designers."

The celebration began precisely at 6:00 p.m., one minute after the waitstaff hit the floor. Edith whispered, "Yes," as a tall, lithe gentleman in tails walked toward their table. He smiled; hands clasped behind his back as he introduced himself.

"Good evening, ladies. My name is William, and I'll be your server. Tonight, we're pleased to offer your choice of seared bluefin tuna, Kobe steak, or sautéed hop shoots and Matsutake mushroom salad. We serve all with garlic roasted La Bonnotte potatoes alongside Yamashita spinach tossed in Lambda olive oil with a Giuseppe Giusti Balsamic Vinaigrette. May I start you off with a bowl of shark fin and sea scallop soup, or perhaps some organic green zebra tomatoes, coated in panko breadcrumbs and fried in truffle oil?"

His upper-class British accent was such a delight to their ears. Glenda waited until he finished before raising her hand. He nodded at her, and she smiled up at him. "Perhaps we might have some cocktails first?"

William bit his lower lip. "Goodness, I'm so sorry. I skipped right over that, didn't I?"

Edith met his gaze. "Don't give it another thought, William. We're here to have a good time, not evaluate your performance and report back to management."

Sharon chimed in, waving her hand in the air. "Yes. We're super chill. I did my time as a waitress back in the day, and it was the hardest job I ever had. You're doing just fine."

Darcy and Glenda nodded, and William sighed in relief. "I can't quite express how much that means to me. It's my first night, and even though I've been in the industry for almost a decade, being a server here is an entirely different level, and I'm rather terrified. I very much appreciate your patience with me. Thank you." He grinned and started over. "So, ladies, what's your poison?"

He returned five minutes later with Glenda's Tom Collins, Darcy's piña colada, Edith's martini, and Sharon's Long Island iced tea. They skipped the appetizers and placed their dinner orders, Sharon and Glenda choosing the Kobe steak, Edith the bluefin tuna, and Darcy the hop shoots and Matsutake mushroom salad. Everything arrived within twenty minutes, and conversation waned as they ate. When William cleared the table, he advised them that dessert would be served after a presentation by the owner of Savannah Valley. Edith stared after him as he walked away.

Sharon rolled her eyes. "A presentation? Before dessert? No one should expect me to pay attention to anything when there's something tasty waiting in the wings."

"I hope they address the fact that what they advertised as Kobe steak was not, I believe, Kobe steak." Glenda shook her head. "Did it taste right to you, Sharon?"

Sharon shrugged. "I've never had Kobe before. Therefore, my opinion is of no consequence." She shifted in her chair to look around the room. "What I'm wondering is where the food came from. All the exterior walls are glass, the elevators are glass, and there are no interior walls, so what gives?"

Edith, midsip of her second martini, held up her left index finger. She spoke as she set her glass down. "Outside, at the far end. There's a pop-up service lift, a huge one the size of a two-car garage. That's where William took the serving cart with our dirty dishes on it." She smirked. "Not that I was watching him walk away. Nope. Not me."

CHAPTER THREE

The Presentation

"Huh, you know what?" Sharon leaned forward, elbows on the table. "I didn't see a button for the fifth floor when we were in the elevator. I wonder if that's where they—" she trailed off as Kool and the Gang's "Celebration" played over the sound system, a stark contrast to the harpist who performed throughout their meal. Three men in designer suits jogged through the dining area, stopping just shy of the folding glass doors. One was blond, the other two brunettes. They had similar hairstyles, short and meticulously coiffed to convey the appearance of not having been attended to at all. The blond, microphone in hand, shouted along with the song lyrics.

"Wahoo! It's a celebration." The other two joined in, clapping and dancing, and the blond shouted into his mic again, attempting to get the residents to join the music. "Come on. Clap along, everybody. This is your time—time to celebrate the rest of your life, the best of your life."

The feeble clapping sounds from around the room faded as the attendees exchanged glances of either confusion or displeasure. The blond ceased his gyrations, and his companions followed suit as the music stopped. He grinned a toothy smile, ignoring the lack of audience participation. "Ladies and gentlemen, my name is Brad Foster-Johnson. As owner and CEO, I'd like to officially welcome you to this community—your community—the most expensive, most *exclusive*, retirement community in the United States—Savannah Valley!"

Brad, again denied any strong reaction from the attendees, stuck to his script as Jensen and another hostess wheeled a ten-foot movie screen behind him. "You're about to see something amazing that I, along with Executive Director Devan Strong, on my left, and General Manager Tyler Wallace, on my right, created not just for you but for the entire world to see. Ready? Here we go."

Brad, Devan, and Tyler stepped aside as the lights dimmed, and an image of an empty piece of land appeared on the screen. Then, a title slid into place from the bottom: Savannah Valley—Making the Rest of Your Life the Best of Your Life. A woman's voice that sounded like a discount version of Apple's Siri narrated as the video progressed.

"Six years ago, Savannah Valley was just a dream. Brad Foster-Johnson's dream. After watching his grandparents move from the family estate into a retirement community, he thought we could surely do better. He asked, 'Why should those who've achieved a certain lifestyle be denied the luxuries they're entitled to when they enter their twilight years?' And the answer was simple:

They shouldn't. Then and there, Brad set his sights on creating a retirement community like no other. And now, that dream has become a reality."

Aerial shots of the property before, during, and after construction scrolled as "Ride of the Valkyries" played in the background. "Set on three thousand acres with only four hundred homes that range in price from six to fifty million dollars, Savannah Valley is the most expensive and most exclusive retirement community in the United States. It features nine five-star restaurants, and each provides delivery service at any time, day or night.

"We staff our gym with on-demand personal trainers, a full-service spa, and indoor and outdoor pools. Other amenities include an eighteen-hole professional golf course, a custom-tailored Whole Foods market, and round-the-clock concierge and housekeeping services. Living in Savannah Valley is like a long-term stay in the world's finest hotel, but with a level of privacy and personalization only your own home can provide."

Edith elbowed Sharon, whispering. "I feel like I'm at one of those awful time-share seminars."

Sharon nodded, raising her eyebrows. "Same for me. Same."

Discount Siri continued, "But there's more. Savannah Valley offers an on-site state-of-the-art medical center to address all your healthcare needs, from wellness visits to emergency procedures. Our pharmacy promises to fill all prescriptions 24/7. Physical and occupational therapists are ready to help you along your road to recovery, should that ever be a need. We've even retained the services of a world-renowned cosmetic surgeon, so you won't have to travel for those nips and tucks."

Glenda whispered, loud enough for others to hear. "It's a lovely idea, but I can't imagine putting myself in the hands of anyone other than Leonard, who I've been going to for the last twenty years." A gentleman two tables away shushed her as the next slide appeared on the screen.

A woman in a floral-print muumuu leaned on a cane while "Blue Hawaii" played in the background. "If mobility becomes an issue, or everyday tasks are challenging, a luxury apartment awaits you in our state-of-the-art assisted living complex, Savannah Valley Sunset. These units are designed to house you and your certified support companion within the same residence while providing privacy and an extra level of service. We can customize each unit to accommodate your unique needs using the most technologically advanced equipment money can buy."

The slideshow ended with a series of photographs beginning with a young couple at their wedding, followed by a middle-aged couple with children, an older couple holding hands, a woman alone, and ending with a group of seniors smiling and laughing in front of the Tower.

The lights came back on, and Brad stepped in front of the podium, grinning as he raised the microphone to his mouth. "If you didn't before, I hope that after seeing our presentation, every one of you understands what an excellent decision you made by choosing Savannah Valley as your new home. Everything you could possibly require, or desire, is right here. So, once more, welcome to Savannah Valley, where you'll be making the rest of your lives the best of your lives."

With that, Brad passed the mic to Devan, then jogged back across the room and dashed into the nearest open elevator. The women exchanged glances. From Devan's and Tyler's expressions, it was clear they hadn't anticipated the abrupt departure of their fearless leader.

Devan nodded as he unbuttoned his royal-blue suit jacket. He tapped on the mic, then leaned forward to speak. "Is this thing on?" His question garnered a few laughs. "I guess that's a yes. Hey, wasn't it great of Brad to join us for this super special occasion? It sure was. He's a busy one, that guy. Always thinking about what's next." He cleared this throat. Scanning the audience, Devan continued. "That brings me to what's next for you: dessert! And on the menu tonight is chocolate cake, but not just any chocolate cake. Chef Marco prepared his decadent creation with the world's rarest cocoa beans, Pure Nacional Fortunato No. 4. The cake is topped with a ganache made from Le

Grand Louis XVI dark chocolate. Every bar contains 99% cocoa. Napoleon loved it, and you will too. The ganache is flecked with bits of edible 14-karat gold, and a champagne-dipped chocolate-coated saffron crocus flower will serve as a garnish." He gestured to his right. "Speaking of champagne, during dessert, your waitstaff will circulate with glasses of Moet & Chandon Esprit du Siecle Brut. Tyler and I will come around to visit as well. Some of you have already spoken with us, but we want to be sure you have the opportunity to ask us anything when we drop by your table."

Devan and Tyler headed off in opposite directions toward either end of the room, and the waitstaff reappeared, carrying large trays of plated cake. The dessert forks were 14-karat gold, with a strip of tiny diamonds running the length of the handle. Darcy broke off a piece of her saffron crocus flower, put it on top of a huge forkful of cake, then stuffed it in her mouth. Still chewing, she spoke. "Mmm. The cake is very rich, and the ganache is bitter." She paused to swallow. "And the saffron is sweet, with just the right amount of floral tones. They absolutely should have served this before the presentation."

Sharon took a bite of her slice. "Oh, I agree. I might have gotten up and danced. *So* good."

Jensen delivered their champagne, and Glenda raised her glass. "A toast to us, living our best lives. We've earned it, ladies." As they clinked their flutes together, Tyler arrived at the table, stroking his patchy beard.

"Good evening, ladies. Gosh, yours is the only table with more than two people. Did you all decide to move here together? That's so *Golden Girls*. I love it."

Sharon leaned in and whispered to Edith. "Good God, who put beards on these children?"

Edith chuckled as Glenda shifted in her seat, straightening her back. "Tyler, I have a question for you about the Kobe steak."

He grinned. "Sure thing. Always happy to help in any way I can."

Glenda smiled in return, clasping her hands in front of her. "I appreciate your enthusiasm and dedication. My question is, are you certain the steak was indeed Kobe? It didn't taste like Kobe to me."

Tyler nodded. "One-hundred-percent certain. From Japanese Black cattle, raised right here in Georgia. Essentially farm to table. I ordered it myself. Perhaps something you ate earlier lingered and affected your palate?"

Glenda's right eyebrow lifted in a scowl. "Young man, I've eaten Kobe beef in Manhattan's most popular Michelin three-star restaurants on multiple occasions, and my palate, which, by the way, is exceptional, detected no difference between them. You've confirmed my suspicions with your comments. For beef from Japanese Black cattle to be certified as Kobe, it must meet stringent standards, one of which is that the cattle must be born in Japan, specifically in the Hyōgo Prefecture. What they served us is domestic Wagyu, not Kobe. You might want to ask for your money back from that supplier if they advertised it as Kobe. I'm afraid you've been deceived."

Tyler forced a smile. "Thank you for that information, and please accept my apology. I'll reach out to my supplier first thing tomorrow and set things straight to make sure this never happens again." He turned and walked away without further comment, but the people at the surrounding tables suddenly had lots to say.

Edith reached out to pat Glenda's hand. "I am impressed by your depth of knowledge and your desire to ensure we're getting what we pay for. Plus, I'm always a big fan of anyone who can dish out a well-deserved fact-based smackdown." She glanced at Darcy and Sharon. "And now I'm curious to learn more about all of you, which, believe me, I did not expect. No offense, ladies. Usually, I can't be bothered because people are horrifically boring, or I just don't like them. Sometimes both." The ladies laughed, and Edith continued. "But you three, I can't put my finger on it. But I think I might actually *like* you. At least for now."

Sharon snorted. "Could it be we're like the *Golden Girls* after all?"

Edith's gaze shifted to William, who was squatting next to another table across the room. She bit her lip, then grinned. "Well, I guess I'll be the token man-eater. Should I change my name to 'Blanche'?"

They turned to see what captured her attention. Glenda lifted from her seat to get a better view. "Hmm, I think I'm going to have to disagree with you there. You're not the only man-eater at the table."

Darcy cleared her throat. "Same here. That boy is beautiful. Did you see those aquamarine eyes? Hoo-wee!"

Sharon remained silent until the other ladies stared at her, waiting for a response. She sighed. "Fine. He's very pretty. Happy? But there goes our chance for our television series unless we call it 'Creaky Cougars.' I don't know about you, but my behind is killing me from sitting in this chair. Anyone game for hanging out tomorrow, preferably somewhere that has cushioned seating?"

They nodded in agreement, and Glenda suggested they have lunch at her place. "And I assure you, whatever I serve will be precisely what I say it is."

While leaving Sky, they noticed a crowd had gathered around Tyler, questioning the authenticity of the contents of their meal, and complaining about the pre-dessert presentation. One person was overheard commenting that the presentation was unnecessary because they already knew everything it contained. Another took issue with the choice to include a sales pitch when this was supposed to be a celebratory event.

Upon exiting the Tower, the valet sheepishly informed Sharon that he had left her key fob inside the Cybertruck by accident. To calm his embarrassment, she put her hand on his shoulder. “I’ve done it before myself. Not to worry, I can open the doors with my phone or fingerprint.”

Before they went separate ways, they confirmed they would meet at Glenda’s at noon the following day. And though no one said it aloud, it was apparent they each felt a level of excitement about their lunch date. It was something none of them had experienced in a long time.

CHAPTER FOUR

Rich Widow Glenda

Old Oak Way, the street farthest from the entrance of Savannah Valley, comprised only forty homes, each set on five-acre parcels that backed to the golf course. Glenda's residence was one of the most expensive high-end properties in the community. A hundred-foot driveway led to a circular turnaround with a garden in its center, and the house itself was a six-thousand-square-foot, two-story modern take on plantation-style structure. There were no columns or exterior stairs, but instead, a recessed courtyard center section served as the grand entrance, the oversized arched glass double doors providing an open view straight through to the backyard. All homes in Savannah Valley were required to adhere to the same color scheme: beige exteriors with dark grey roofs, all chosen from a preapproved palette of four nearly indistinguishable shades. However, the architectural aspects were more flexible and reviewed on a case-by-case basis, with homes not visible from the street permitted the most design freedoms.

Edith, Sharon, and Darcy arrived at Glenda's, sharing Darcy's Onward Club Car golf cart. Savannah Valley provided every homeowner with one, and using them instead of traditional vehicles was strongly encouraged by management as part of the community's "Keep SV Green"

initiative. The carts were lithium-ion battery powered and came with an onboard Connect system that mapped the entire property. They equipped each to be used to shop, make dinner reservations, or even order takeout for delivery to wherever the cart was currently located. As they parked off to the right of the circle near the charging station and began walking toward the home, Glenda stepped outside to greet them.

"Hello, ladies. Welcome to Old Oak Way." She held the door ajar as they approached. "Come on in. I'll have you know that, other than staff, you're the first to see the place, so pretend to be impressed."

As they walked through the foyer, Darcy pointed at a painting hanging on the cream-colored wall to their right. "If that's an actual Jackson Pollock, I won't *need* to pretend."

Glenda stopped to look at the piece, a soft smile on her lips, then turned to Darcy. "It is. It's been in storage since I bought it in 1982, and now she's finally home. His work will always hold a special place in my heart."

Darcy repressed the urge to ask if she'd known him, but Sharon couldn't help herself. "Did you know him personally?"

Glenda nodded. "I met him once, but I was just a kid. Let's wait until after lunch to spill our collective beans, shall we? It's Southern fried chicken, and it loses its luster when it's even the slightest bit cold."

They followed Glenda forward as she entered the center of the home, a large circular atrium that quartered the space. She turned left down a hallway that led into an open-style kitchen and dining area. Both were white walled with sparkling gray quartz floors throughout. A dark slate-gray subway tile backsplash highlighted high-gloss dove gray kitchen cabinets with satin-chrome pulls, and the countertops matched the flooring. All appliances, including the range hood and microwave, were from the Big Chill Retro line in their pink lemonade shade. Hanging on the wall at the far end of the sixteen-seat dining table was a huge rectangular painting, abstract in style, featuring red, pink, and gray gradients.

Edith glanced back and forth from the kitchen to the dining room, then pointed at the painting. "Okay, who's up for a wager, ladies? Was the painting purchased to match the space, or was the space designed to match the painting? Fifty bucks say it's the latter."

Sharon shrugged. "Depends on who designed the space. I can't solve the equation if I don't have all the variables."

Glenda chuckled as she took the pan of chicken out of the warming oven and set it on the island counter. "I designed it myself, Sharon. Carry on."

"Well, I'm with Edith then. Space designed to match the painting. What say you, Darcy?"

“Oh, I agree. So, Glenda, do we get to keep our money?”

Nodding, she took four plates out of an upper cabinet and set them next to the pan. “You do. You’re all correct. I designed the space around the painting. It’s called Silver Light, and the artist is Esteban Vicente. Another one that was in storage for a few years.” She opened a drawer to retrieve serving tongs. “Help yourself to some chicken while I retrieve the biscuits out of the oven. Gravy is in the tureen on the dining table, as are napkins, utensils, and glasses. I made collard greens with bacon as well. I hope you all like sweet tea. Happy to add some hard stuff to it if you wish.”

They sat across from each other, complimenting Glenda on her culinary skills throughout. She served homemade peach pie for dessert, and after cleaning up, the ladies retreated to the living room with their coffees. It was at the rear right of the home, with large arched windows providing a view of the backyard garden and the green space beyond. Light beige walls and Sahara gold marble tile complimented the Mariner Gatsby cream-colored sofas arranged opposite each other to create a circular conversation space. Four black lacquered end tables held a Tiffany Woodbine lamp, and a round matching coffee table rested in the middle. Glenda and Edith chose the sofa that faced the windows, with Darcy and Sharon sitting opposite them.

Sharon sighed happily. "My wish for cushioned seating has been granted. This couch is spectacular, Glenda. I love the whole art deco vibe. And all the art in general. How long have you been a collector?"

"I didn't start collecting until after my husband passed away, but I've always been incredibly passionate about art." She took a deep breath, then continued. "Sorry about that. Saying it out loud is rather new to me. I suppressed that passion for a very long time but being able to display my collection has, well, I'm not sure what it's done, but it makes me feel like I've taken a step toward circling back to who I used to be. Perhaps even who I was meant to be." She shook her head as if to clear it. "And now I'm waxing philosophical on you all. Good lord."

Darcy leaned forward, eyes full of anticipation. "Glenda, I'm enjoying the waxing. Please, elaborate. Who is Glenda Edelman? Her story is one I can't wait to hear. Maybe one I *need* to hear."

Glenda, blushing, covered her mouth with her right hand as she waved the left at Darcy. "You flatter me. And I appreciate your kindness." She balled her hands into fists, raised her elbows, then lowered them as she brought her fists together in front of her chest. "All right then, here we go. So, who is Glenda Edelman, the CliffsNotes version."

They all laughed, and Glenda took another deep breath, then began. "I was born in 1941, in the Bronx. My parents, the Walshes, emigrated from Ireland in 1938. My father opened an ice cream shop on Fordham Road in 1946, and I helped there from when I was eight all the way through until I graduated from high school in 1959. I'd excelled at mathematics and received a full engineering scholarship to the Cooper Institute. Much to the horror of my parents, I accepted it. It's the Cooper Union now, still located in Greenwich Village. During my first semester there, I connected with several art student majors, and I switched my major to art in my second semester."

"That must have been a shock to the family," Darcy said.

"My parents stopped speaking to me at that point, but I didn't bat an eyelash. I fell in love with the Village, its art, its culture, its everything. We were the Beat generation, the rejectors of materialism and mainstream values. We wanted our art—whether drawn, spoken, played, or sung—to elevate consciousness and be accessible to everyone. My medium was paint on canvas, paint on paper, paint on walls, paint on anything it would cling to."

"That explains a lot about your exquisite collection, Glenda."

"I lived on coffee and cigarettes, barely sleeping because there was just so much to do. I felt I had so much to learn and so much to experience. I met Jack Kerouac and Allen Ginsberg in 1963—both on the same night at a

warehouse party where I was on stage painting live. It was the best of times."

She smiled, nodding slowly. "On that same night, at that same party, I met the man who would become my husband: Percy Edelman. He was forty-two, twenty years older than I was, and still a bachelor. He was born into wealth, his family's fortune made in real estate, insurance, and railroads, which I despised. But my God, was he gorgeous. Black curly hair, green eyes, six feet of perfectly sculpted man that moved with cat-like grace. Despite him saying that I was 'the one' and that he'd never encountered a woman he'd wanted to settle down and raise a family with before, I was deeply concerned about the disparity between our value systems. I didn't want to surrender my freedom of expression, or my freedom, period. It took four years of his constant reassurance that he didn't expect nor want me to change to get me to agree to marry him. We wed in 1967 in Manhattan, where he'd grown up, and moved into a three-floor apartment on Fifth Avenue that overlooked Central Park."

Glenda stopped to sip her coffee, then continued. "Of course, that was all a lie. I found out three months in that he was married before but divorced her because she couldn't have children. He bought her an apartment on the West Side and paid her half a million to keep it quiet. A month later, two days after I decided to leave him, I found out I was pregnant. And when *he* found out, that was the end of my artistic endeavors. I was to be Mrs. Edelman, wife and mother, and nothing more from that point forward.

She put her cup down before continuing. "The twins, Thomas and Percy Jr., were born in 1968. Stanley was born in 1970, and Kathleen in 1972. I was thirty-one with four kids under the age of five, and though we had a day maid, all the remaining household responsibilities fell to me. I know I have no right to complain because we were very well-off and wanted for nothing, but that became part of the problem. Once they were school-aged, Percy let the kids have whatever they wanted, whenever they wanted it. I had no authority. If I said 'no,' the kids would go to him, and he'd tell them, of course, they could, and that they didn't have to listen to me. It created a huge disconnect between us, and to be honest, I gave in and gave up on raising socially conscious, fiscally responsible children."

She stood and walked to the window. "Taking part in high-society activities and events with other wives was encouraged, so I attended events and parties. I hosted afternoon tea for all the other bored, rich women at least once a week. We fundraised, sponsored galas, had front-row opening night seats to all the best Broadway shows, ate at the finest restaurants, and made sure we turned up wherever everyone who was anyone would be—hence, the Halston showing. It was all very competitive, each of us trying to one-up each other for clout, but keeping busy kept me sane. So did Percy's nonstop travel schedule. He was only home one or two weekends a month, which was perfectly fine with me. I did my thing, he did his, and that was that. We fulfilled our familial holiday and social obligations together, but aside from that, we lived separate lives."

Turning back to the women, Glenda continued. "That changed in 1994 when he was diagnosed with dementia. I was his primary caregiver for the next six years—largely because he didn't want anyone to know about his condition. By early 2001, it was impossible to hide it any longer, and I'd just begun the process of finding an assisted-living facility when he got the kids involved. They didn't want him, and I quote, 'put in some disgusting place with a bunch of regular people' when I had nothing better to do than take care of him. They agreed that an in-home aide was acceptable as long as we installed security cameras to make sure everything was on the up-and-up. When he had a massive stroke in 2004, I converted one of our master suites into a hospital room, and we hired nursing staff to be there around the clock. He passed away in 2006."

Edith opened her mouth, then closed it again. After taking a deep breath, she spoke. "Though it's a challenge for me, I'm going to refrain from speaking disparagingly about your offspring. But I'm very sorry that happened to you."

Glenda laughed. "Edith, I wish I could say the same for myself, but then I'd be a bad parent *and* a liar. I do appreciate your sentiment very much. Thank you for that. But don't feel too bad. Our wills were drawn up right after we were married, and he never bothered to add the kids as beneficiaries. Everything he owned, all his assets, every single last cent, went to me. All four billion dollars and change of it."

She paused, and though she didn't expect any, waited a beat for reactions. There were none, and she resumed. "The children, as you would expect, were not pleased. I gave each of them fifty million dollars, then revised my will so that whatever remains when I pass will be distributed among them equally. They were still not pleased. I was reasonably frugal until I turned seventy-two, and the 'maybe it's time to downsize' conversation occurred. That's when I dipped my toe back into the art world by collecting. They found out about it a year and a half ago, and they staged an intervention at my daughter's home intending to convince me I could no longer manage my finances on my own and thus should consider giving them power of attorney."

She walked back to her seat and topped off her coffee cup. "I laughed and told them I knew their motivation had nothing to do with my well-being. It was all about how they could ensure the most money possible would be left when I

kicked the bucket. So, I decided I was going to liquidate all my assets and try my darndest to spend every penny just to spite them. And that, ladies, is how I ended up in Savannah Valley in a ridiculously expensive house that's entirely too big for one person and filled with ridiculously expensive things—all of which, by the way, I believe I've earned and deserve." Sharon started to speak, but Glenda cut her off. "I think we should save our comments for another time. After having shared my story, I'm eager to hear everyone else's. Is that all right?"

The ladies nodded, and Glenda pointed at Edith. "Given my experience with a single instance of wedded non-bliss, I must know in what circumstance one would endure being married more than once."

CHAPTER FIVE

Rich Widow Edith

Edith's laugh echoed in the large open space. "Listen, men are like bras. You see one that's pretty, it suits your style, it's made from your favorite material, and it's available in your normally hard-to-find size. It's love at first sight. This one, *this* is the bra for me. So, you buy it. But sometimes, when you get it home and try it on, it's just not right. It might not lift things up as expected, dig into your skin, give you side boob, show under your form-fitting garments, squeeze the breath out of you, but you *want* to keep loving it, so you keep wearing it, and for a while, you tell yourself that the problem is you, not the bra."

She cupped her hands under her breasts. "And then, one day, when you find yourself fiddling with the darn thing, like sneaking into the coatroom so you can reach in and adjust the girls for the millionth time because you're trying so hard to make it work, you can't take it anymore, and you say 'wow, screw this thing.' So, you take it off and go braless for the rest of the day, and yeah, you feel like a pariah for an hour or so, not because men are looking at you, which is to be expected and enjoyed, but because women are, too, and they're judging you. But then, you hit

bralless nirvana. You realize that this is natural, this feels amazing, this is the way you were meant to live."

Edith let out a roaring laugh and pointed to her chest. "And you remain sans bra day in and day out until you start to wonder: Is this the way I was meant to live? Will this make my boobs sag faster? Will I end up lighting one or both of my nipples on fire while I'm making bacon and eggs for breakfast? Before you know it, you start looking at bras again, just for the purpose of research and consideration, and then there it is, another bra, and it's stunning. Then, there *you* are, going full-on Britney Spears because, oops, you did it again."

Glenda, Sharon, and Darcy were laughing hysterically, tears and all.

Edith gave them a few minutes to regain their composure before continuing. "If you thought that was funny, wait until I tell you what career path I ended up on—divorce attorney."

The ladies screeched, dissolving into laughter once again, Edith along with them. Once the intermittent bursts of giggles ceased, Edith resumed speaking.

"I was a heck of a good one, too, even though it wasn't what I thought I'd be doing. I made partner in my firm when I was thirty-five, only two years out of law school. Right after high school, I attended Boston University's College of Fine Arts. That's where I'm originally from,

Boston. The family roots go back to the 1600s, and there were some financial success stories along the way, but my branch was always middle-class or below. I grew up poor, my father drank, yadda yadda."

She paused for reaction but when none came, she continued. "You've heard those kinds of stories a thousand times already. I was awarded a full scholarship, got my BA in theater and my master's in directing. Finding a job in Boston was pretty much impossible, so I moved to New York City and started at the bottom. There was a lot of off-Broadway and understudy work before I landed a role in *Cats* in 1986 playing Electra. Two weeks after my first performance, I was crossing the street in Times Square and got hit by a taxi, shattered my kneecap, and that was that. Back to Boston I went, and six months later, I married my physical therapist, Jeff. We divorced in 1988 after he cheated on me with another client. I sat around being bitter for the better part of a year, then decided to sell the house I'd been awarded in the settlement and use the money to go to law school."

She tapped her index finger to her lip as though pondering her next statement. "Courtrooms are essentially theaters when you think about it. The judge is the director; the plaintiff, the defendant, and their respective legal teams are the performers; and the jury members are the critics.

Sometimes there's even an audience. The rush when you win is just as powerful, perhaps even more so than when you receive a standing ovation. I can't tell you if losing is as tragically disappointing as being booed because, though I settled plenty of cases, I never ever lost one."

She paused, reflecting for a moment as she recalled how it felt to hear the thud of the judge's gavel before announcing a decision in her favor. "There were three more husbands after that, Chris and Steve, the former decent but not very ambitious, the latter very ambitious, but a self-absorbed bozo who thought the world revolved around him and him alone. A firm in LA offered me a position as partner in 2009, so I moved out to the West Coast. For my first high-profile case, I represented Julie Ibarra, wife of big-time studio exec Marco Ibarra. No, I can't say the name of the studio because there's an NDA in place, but feel free to Google it later. She cited abandonment because he traveled constantly and worked such long hours, and after six months of back and forth, he finally agreed to a seven-figure settlement."

"It sounds like she deserved every penny of that and more," Sharon enthused.

"Two weeks after everything was signed, he stopped by the office and asked if he could take me out to lunch. When I said, 'no thanks,' he smiled and said that was just what he expected, complimented my tenacity, intelligence, and negotiation tactics, called me a force to be reckoned with, and left. A month later, I pulled Julie's file to get his number and asked him to lunch. He accepted, and a week later, we married at the Graceland Wedding Chapel in Las Vegas. We had a pretty good run, honestly. Maybe it was because we were older. I was fifty when we met; he was sixty-five. Maybe it was because he treated me with respect and admired the personality traits I possess—the same ones that others thought were too masculine, too strong, or just too much. Or maybe it was that I respected *him*, which was, truth be told, totally new for me."

Darcy jumped in, "It sounds like you found a winner."

She let out a deep sigh. "Hmph, like all good things, like all things in general, it didn't last. In 2015, he had a heart attack while we were doing the horizontal mambo. Before he went in for surgery, he told me he loved me and said that if he died, I should know that he thought having mind-blowing sex with his gorgeous wife was absolutely the only way to go. Those ended up being his last words."

She brushed a tear off her cheek, then smiled. "He left me seven-hundred-fifty million dollars and a note that read 'My dearest Edie, Go. Do what you love. Be who you are.' I'm still trying to figure out what he meant by that, but I knew I wanted to get as far away from LA as possible but still be in a warm climate. Savannah won out as the most acceptable location, so here I am, drifting in a sea of cluelessness concerning what I'm supposed to do with the rest of my life. Rich beyond what I could ever have imagined, but still drifting and clueless. Darcy, your turn."

CHAPTER SIX

Rich Widow Darcy

Darcy got up, walked across to where Edith was sitting, bent down to hug her, then returned to her seat next to Sharon. She cleared her throat, then spoke. "I grew up in Rockaway, New Jersey. Kind of rural, kind of a suburb, and only thirty-five miles from New York City. My father was an Army sergeant during World War II, and my mother was a USO girl. She was born and raised in Rockaway, too, and he was from Pittsburgh, but they met in London right after the war ended. We were middle class through and through. All about block parties, potluck dinners, football games, barbecues—all that pre-Vietnam Americana goodness. By the time I graduated from high school in 1967, ten of my classmates had enlisted or were drafted."

Her eyes drifted upward as if their images were painted on the ceiling. "Only four made it back. Whenever the news covered antiwar or antidraft stories or protests, my father would leap out of his recliner, turn off the television, and go off on a tirade about what a bunch of anti-American sissies my generation was. One did not dare to disagree with my father's beliefs on *any* topic in our house, so I remained silent. When I expressed an interest in studying

fashion design, he resisted but finally agreed to let me go to college. But only if I studied nursing instead, an 'appropriate woman's profession,' in his words, and I had to still live at home. In April 1969, we learned that Ricky, my younger brother who had enlisted in the Marines when he graduated from high school in 1968, was killed in action."

Sharon pressed a hand on Darcy's knee which seemed to squeeze a few unshed tears from her eyes. "My mother was completely broken, my father stoic and proud to have raised such a hero. I coped by shifting all my focus to finishing my degree, and during the summer, I worked at a local bakery to keep myself busy. It seemed like every day brought news of the death of someone else we knew, so my friends and I attended rallies and protests at local colleges. Over the Fourth of July weekend, my father discovered what I'd been doing. He threw me out of the house. I couch surfed until we left for Bethel, New York, on August 14 to attend the Woodstock Music and Art Fair."

She swiped her cheek and grinned widely. "During Richie Havens' set, I noticed this guy in front of me. Skinny with blond hair that just brushed his shoulders, wearing only a pair of jeans. He was dancing like a madman, whirling and twirling, and he kept sneaking glances at me. When Richie finished singing "Freedom," the guy stopped dancing, pushed his way through the crowd, took my hands in his, and said, 'I'm Greg Peterson. Come with me to San

Francisco.' His eyes were so blue and so kind. I said 'sure,' and after Woodstock was done, off we went. He drove a black 1964 Mustang convertible, which he sold when we got to San Francisco, so we could rent a studio apartment in Haight-Ashbury. It was a real dump, but we didn't care.

"I always regretted not going to Woodstock," Glenda said wistfully.

Darcy closed her eyes, and the memory flooded her face. "We were young, we were in love, and we were right in the center of a social upheaval that we hoped would change our country forever. Everything was in my name so Greg couldn't be traced. I got a job at Saint Mary's Hospital, and he did odd jobs that paid in cash. Things began to fall apart pretty quickly when people started doing hard drugs though. By 1971, we'd saved up enough money to buy a used van we could live in and cover expenses for a year, so we lit out and followed the Grateful Dead around."

Sharon leaned forward, mouth agape. "No, you did not."

Darcy chuckled. "Oh yes, we did. Greg and I embraced the hippie lifestyle. After that first year, we stayed in a commune, and I discovered the magic of living off the land. Everything we needed we could grow: food, medicine, clothing. I was obsessed with herbalism. I never felt so alive. I could have stayed there forever, or at least that's how I felt until I got pregnant.

We'd been trying for a while, and I was at the point where I figured it wasn't meant to be. Then—boom! I tossed my cookies on the poor girl in front of me right in the middle of "Box of Rain" at a Dead concert. I couldn't envision myself with a baby in a sling while I toked on a joint and picked corn, so we decided it was probably best to rejoin society."

She lifted her coffee cup, then put it down again. "Greg grew up in Greenwich, Connecticut, and his older brother, Barry, offered him a job as a stockbroker at the firm he managed in Manhattan. So, we headed back East and moved in with my mother. My father had passed away in 1972, and she was thrilled to have some life back in the house. Daisy, my daughter, was born on the first day of spring in 1975. I stayed home with her for the first year while Greg commuted into the city every day. And, my God, was I bored. Staying home and taking care of a child day in and day out just wasn't for me."

This time when she picked up the cup, she sipped the cold coffee and pressed her lips together. "Mom noticed how miserable I was, so she offered to use some of the money from Dad's life insurance settlement to pay for me to go back to college. I was finally able to study fashion design while Mom babysat Daisy. In 1977, they offered me an internship at *Vogue*, and of course, I jumped at the chance. That led to a paid position as a merchandise

planner, and by 1983, I worked my way up to trend forecaster. Greg and I were making upward of three-hundred thousand a year together, but the commute was brutal. So, we made the difficult decision to leave Rockaway behind and bought our apartment in London Terrace, in Chelsea."

"You had quite a life, Darcy." Edith leaned forward. "Tell us the rest."

"That was a wild time, the eighties. We hired a full-time live-in person to cook, clean, and take care of Daisy, so we could work overtime and then go out and party with our colleagues. There was this sense of incredible selfishness all around us. Self-importance, everyone's worthiness, was determined by how much they made and the value of the material possessions they accumulated. I'll never understand how Greg and I got sucked into that mindset, but we did and somehow thrived in the midst of it."

Restless, she stood and walked behind the sofa as if delivering a lecture. "The fashion business was cutthroat, and being a stockbroker was that and then some. It brought out a side of Greg that I didn't particularly like. But it was his ability to climb up and over anyone and anything in his path that helped his firm to survive the Black Monday market crash in 1987 and again in 2008. He turned 60 that year, and that's when he began to question. I'd begun my own questioning in 2005, when I decided to shift from being directly involved in the fashion industry to curating for museums and private collectors. Greg left his firm in 2010 to work as a private consultant helping clients build their retirement portfolios."

She moved back to her seat and rested her head against the pillow closing her eyes. "Both of us planned to keep working until we turned 70, at which point we'd retire and relocate to Georgia. In December 2017, we took a road trip to check out some spots down here, and on the way home, someone ran a red light and T-boned us. I walked away without a scratch, but Greg was killed instantly. He was 69."

She tilted her head forward and stared at the floor, then looked back up, squaring her shoulders before she spoke. "We had a hundred million in the bank, and between his life insurance and the accident settlement, I ended up with a net worth of over five hundred million. Daisy lives here in Savannah with her husband Stefan and their four kids I've never met. After college, she went her way, and we grew more and more estranged. Our contact was limited to exchanging cards and photos for birthdays and holidays. We weren't invited to her wedding. She didn't come to his funeral. And you know, I don't blame her one bit. We were too busy chasing money to raise her as we should have. She barely saw us, and when she did, we were never in the moment. We were always thinking about what was next instead. We bought her anything her heart desired, but never gave her our time." The words tumbled from her mouth.

She looked at each of the women, then added, "And that's the one thing that you can't buy more of, you know? Time. Not yet anyway. When Greg died, I took a good hard look at myself and wondered what happened to that woman who wanted to live *freely*—free from material possessions, free from society's expectations, free from the endless cycle of consumerism. I wondered what the heck had happened to my *soul*. But at the same time, I knew I didn't want to go back. I didn't want to leave behind all Greg and I worked so hard for, everything we built together, and find a commune or something."

"This must have been so awful for you," Glenda said.

Darcy smiled and shrugged her shoulders. "I like having the funds to do what I want when I want. I enjoy modern conveniences. And designer clothes. And meat. I guess what I'm looking for now is balance. I'm hoping that when I find that balance, I can muster up enough courage to ask my daughter to forgive me. I would never expect that from her, but perhaps she will allow us to get to know each other again, to get to know each other period. We never really did, and that's the one thing in my life I'd change if I had the chance. That's why I'm here. This is my last stop. I'll either get it done or die trying." Jaw firmly set, she nodded and patted Sharon's knee.

CHAPTER SEVEN

Rich Widow Sharon

Sharon glanced at Darcy, then down at the floor. She took a long, shaky breath, then looked up and over at Glenda and Edith. "I, um, I'm . . . wow, I didn't think it would be this hard to, you know, *talk*. About it. About *him*." She closed her eyes, took another deep breath, then opened them before continuing. "Okay. Sorry. I guess I'll just start and see where it goes."

Darcy leaned in and put her arm around Sharon's shoulder and gave her a gentle squeeze. Edith smiled and pointed at Darcy. "Uh-oh. It looks like we have a hugger in our midst, ladies."

Darcy shot her a glance. "All you need is love, you know."

Glenda snorted. "Having tons of money in the bank doesn't hurt either."

They all laughed, which gave Sharon the boost she needed to share her story. "Eighteen months and seventeen days. That's how long it's been since I lost Roger." She shook her head. "I keep saying 'lost' like I left him somewhere and can't find him. Which I guess is sort of true, but also completely *not* true. I should say 'died.' Eighteen months and seventeen days since Roger *died*. But I don't want to say that because it makes so much more *real*." She paused, took a deep breath, then smiled. "He'd be super annoyed with me for staring in the rearview again. He always focused on planning cool stuff for me to do after he was gone, and that was what gave him some peace at the end."

The smile turned to a frown as she struggled to hold back tears. "Pancreatic cancer. Diagnosed in 2015. He was only 44. Some people thought it was strange that Roger was 5 years younger than me. Some of his buddies warned him from the beginning that he should reconsider his affection for me. That I would be old and decrepit when he was still young and vital. So much for that unsolicited advice.

"The first three years weren't so bad, but that last one, he was so calm and accepting of it all, always way more concerned about how I was doing. I think that was the hardest part for me, other than knowing he would be leaving me. I pretended I was fine and dandy when, inside, I was a storm of blind rage and infinite sorrow. I didn't want him to ever see it, so I tried to hide it, but I'm sure he knew anyway. We were so close, and we were always honest with each other. I can't imagine I pulled off lying to him." She wept openly.

Darcy gave her another squeeze. "He sounds like he was an amazing fellow, Sharon. I'm so very sorry for your loss." The other ladies echoed her sentiment, then remained silent as they allowed Sharon time to regroup. Glenda left the room and came back with a box of tissues and a very large black cat she plopped unceremoniously onto Sharon's lap.

"Sharon, this is Salvador. Once you get a look at his face, you'll know why. He's my living Tiger Balm, soothes every ache and pain with his purry snuggles." She reached down and scratched his chin, causing him to raise his head.

Sharon, cheeks still wet with tears, laughed loudly. "Oh my God, look at that white mustache. He's like a reverse Dali in cat form." She dabbed at her nose with a tissue, then petted him, stroking from head to tail. "Hey there, buddy. What's up, my little kitty boy?"

Salvador purred loudly, stood, turned in a circle, then draped himself across Sharon's thighs as he made digging motions with his front paws. Sharon grinned, elbowing Darcy.

"Look, we have *air biscuits*. Woo-hoo." She looked up at Glenda. "Thank you for this. I'm like a crazy cat lady-in-waiting. Roger and I had five between us when we met, but our last passed right before Roger got sick. I was waiting until I got settled to find a new friend. Salvador is an awesome preview. Also, I'm probably going to be visiting him, oops, I mean you, every single day from now on, or at least until I adopt my new fur baby. No joke."

Glenda smiled. "I do believe Salvador would enjoy that very much."

Sharon kissed the tips of her left index and middle fingers, then patted Salvador's head with them. "Good.

It's settled then." She glanced around at the three women, all unknown to her until yesterday, to whom she'd freely spoken aloud the things that she'd held inside herself for so long. Too long. She smiled, then continued her story. "Okay. Enough with the tragedy. Time for a brief history of Sharon McAlister Wright, the woman who took great pleasure in making computer and gaming industry dudes feel uncomfortable and inadequate throughout the entirety of her career, born and raised in the Chestnut Hill section of Philadelphia."

Edith leaned forward, nodding. "Oh, I like the sound of this, Sharon. I like it a *lot*."

Sharon grinned. "I'd be disappointed if you didn't, Edith. So. Anyhow. My dad's family came over from Scotland after World War I. They settled in Philly and set up shop in the fish market. I have cousins who are still running the place. Dad met Mom in 1963 at a memorial ceremony for JFK. He provided the seafood for the buffet. They got married in 1964, and two years later, I entered the picture. He started working for Radio Shack in 1967, and she got a job in the accounting department at Woolworths when I started school. They divorced when I was eleven, but it was as amicable. Well, as amicable as a divorce can get, I guess. Dad got an apartment downtown, so he'd be close, and I spent weekends and summers at his place. He bought me a TRS-80 computer for my twelfth birthday, showed me how to enter the code to make my name repeat and scroll on the screen, and that was that. I was hooked."

She paused, lost in the memory. "By the time I graduated from high school, I was building my own homebrew machines, and I landed a full scholarship to Drexel University to study computer science. Only lasted two years, though, because when Windows came out in 1985, I decided that if Bill Gates could quit Harvard and make something so amazing, Drexel could kiss my butt goodbye."

A low chuckle, almost a growl escaped Sharon's lips. "So, I packed all my worldly belongings into my Ford Escort and headed for Palo Alto, California. I found a room to rent in a dilapidated old Victorian house full of other computer nerds gone rogue, and six months later, I managed to get my foot in the door of SRI International. I was privileged to be the only female participant in a project that resulted in the birth of the internet." She paused, glancing at the ladies. "I mean, in reality, *they* all knew they were privileged to have *me* on board, but they would have rather gotten kicked in their nether regions by a Clydesdale than admit it."

Edith shook her head, a broad grin covering her face, she raised her fist in the air. "Say it, sister."

Sharon gave her a thumbs up. "Loud and proud. All these years later, you know, it's better. But the fact that it's still a *thing*, well, don't even get me started. But, onward.

My housemates began writing computer games, and I was their go-to for problem solving. When the games went online, I stepped into the role of network management and security, at which point I left SRI and started freelancing. It was ridiculously lucrative. It was all very new, and virus and network protection software were always five steps behind the hackers, so businesses were throwing cash at anyone who could lock their stuff down. The irritation of their initial hesitation about hiring a chick and constant questioning of my abilities aside, it was the easiest money I ever made. I kind of had a god complex going for a little while.

She shifted in her seat. "That's when I got into playing games instead of helping write them because I lacked the agility skill set required to be more than mediocre at it. Want to get knocked off your high horse? Have some eleven-year-old kick your butt at a game you helped code. But it turned out to be much more than humbling. It was a *huge* lightbulb moment for me. I'd always just been the fixer, never the player, but experiencing things from the end-user side allowed me to see what was missing, as well as the endless possibilities that could be achieved with each leap forward in computer hardware."

"I don't know anything about gaming, but it sounds like fun." Glenda scratched her nose.

"Oh, it is. I cut way back on freelancing and made

my own gaming engine. That's, like, the basic framework software that developers use to make their games. I guess, hmm, well, a good analogy is that it serves a similar purpose like a mannequin does for a fashion designer. If you ever hear someone mention the Infinitum engine, that's me. Released in 1995, sold to an American company who shall remain nameless in 2001. I invested half of my savings in Yahoo's IPO in 1996, then the other half in Amazon's IPO in 1997, and suddenly, working was entirely optional for me."

The puzzled looks on the other women's faces made her giggle. "Bear with me. This will all make sense, I hope. It was then that I started entering hacking competitions so I wouldn't get rusty, and that's how I met Roger. It was March 1999, and I was a contestant in the Los Altos MegaCyber Network Security Challenge. No one had ever bested me, but all weekend I'd been hearing about some dude who was just over the top, a total genius. He'd blown through every match in record time and secured his place in the finals three hours before I did. When we faced each other on Sunday night, he shook my hand, pulled out my chair for me, and eight brain-melting hours later, he won. He hacked into the server literally fifteen seconds before I did, but still, he beat me. And, boy, was I furious.

Her animated expression gave a hint about what was coming next. "It took everything I had to get off my chair and congratulate him. But I did, and as we walked toward each other, he tripped over an electrical cord and fell flat on his face. In front of an audience of several thousand people. And on live television. I jogged over and squatted down next to him to ask if he was okay. He lifted himself on his arms and said, 'I feel incredibly slighted that my fifteen minutes of fame will now be associated with me being a clumsy dork as opposed to the genius who finally out-hacked Sharon McAlister. But other than that, I'm fine. Thanks for asking.'"

Sharon folded her napkin and placed it on her knee. "He got back to his feet on his own, and as I rose, our eyes met just for an instant. He looked down at the stage floor, and I watched as this enormous blush worked its way from the neck of his *X-Files* T-shirt straight up to his forehead. His glasses were slightly askew, and without even thinking about it, I reached out to fix them. Which is not something I would ever normally do. And then, as I was still adjusting to the shock of my boldness, he grabbed my hand and lifted our arms in the air."

"Oh, that is so romantic," Darcy swooned.

Sharon continued. "The audience cheered, and as we left the stage, we started talking and kept talking for the next twenty years. Our first official date was dinner at McDonald's, followed by a movie. We went to see *The Matrix* on opening night. He grew up in Seattle, and I moved in with him a month after we met. We got married that October, moved to Philadelphia, and started our own gaming company, Red Pill Productions, in 2001. That was mainly for fun. We made one together that was pretty popular, and I'm still getting royalty checks. All that goes to charity, though."

Her face took on a Mona Lisa wistful smile. "Roger and I made a formidable investment team, and we cashed in on the Google, Twitter, and Facebook IPOs. Right now, I'm sitting on just over a billion, but I don't know, you know? If having it isn't enough to save the person you love most in this world, what's the point? Roger's plan for me was to take his Cybertruck, which he pre-ordered but never actually got to see in person, and travel around the country visiting places we'd never been but held special meaning for us until I found 'the spot.' I scoffed at that idea initially, but after he died, I understood his insistence that I follow through because I couldn't even go back inside our house in Philly."

"I can relate to that. It's hard to go back to a place that has so many memories," Glenda nodded.

Sharon nodded her head too. "I had movers pack everything and put it in storage. Then off I went. Savannah was last on the list, and I stayed at the Bohemian for six weeks because I had no clue what to do next. Then I saw a rental was available here, and I thought, *why the heck not*? The climate's nice, the house is nice, the community's nice, no one knows me, and downtown is the only place I've found so far where I can *feel* him, you know? *Midnight in the Garden of Good and Evil* was the first movie we watched together when I moved into his place, and we made it part of our anniversary tradition. We always meant to visit when we were older and not so busy."

She paused, the corners of her mouth turning up in a slight smile. "I was majorly peeved at first that they moved the Bird Girl statue from the Bonaventure Cemetery, but now, not so much. Whether I stand in front of her at the Jepsen Center or walk the grounds of the cemetery, I'm overwhelmed by this sense of belonging, of peace. It's the way I always felt when I was with him. And those are the moments when I catch a glimpse of a future for myself without him, which is what he wanted for me even though I insisted it would never, ever happen. So here I am, trying to wrap my head around a post-Roger existence. All I'm sure of right now is that I'm honored to be in your company, my fellow widows of Savannah Valley."

Darcy raised her coffee cup in a toast. "As am I, sweetie. A toast to us, the widows of Savannah Valley."

Glenda shook her head. "Something's missing there.

How about a toast to us, the *rich* widows of Savannah Valley?"

Edith nodded. "Hear, hear. To the rich widows of Savannah Valley. May we always have more fun than legally allowed and make a spectacle of ourselves wherever our money takes us."

Sharon lifted her hands in front of her, slowly spreading them apart and upward, palms forward and fingers splayed. "I can see it now, us walking down the streets of Beverly Hills, going in and out of the stores in our matching silk jackets with 'Rich Widows of Savannah Valley' written across the back in diamonds. Giant ones, so anyone walking behind us is blinded by the sparkling."

Darcy snorted. "We'll be like the Pink Ladies from *Grease* if they would have hit it really, really big."

Edith raised her hand. "I'll be Rizzo."

Sharon rolled her eyes. "Wow, what a shocker."

Standing and putting her hands on her hips, Edith sang, "There are worse things I could do than go with a boy or two."

Glenda stood as well. "Yes, like having another slice of peach pie. But this time, à la mode. Who's with me?"

Sharon, Edith, and Darcy shouted "Me!" in unison, and the ladies adjourned to the kitchen.

As Glenda got their second round of dessert ready,

Edith commented that while each one of them had come of age in four different decades, they found common ground through both their shared experiences as women and with personal loss. She hummed another song from Grease, "We Go Together," under her breath as Glenda served them.

Here they were, four rich widows, sitting together in a multimillion-dollar kitchen, enjoying each other's company and some warm peach pie with vanilla bean ice cream. They had no one to answer to but themselves, just living in the moment with essentially limitless possibilities ahead of them.

Edith paused just before taking a second bite of her slice of pie. "You know, I hate to admit this because that Brad guy seems like a complete jerk, and I was deeply offended by some of last night's presentation, but I'm beginning to think he might have been on to something with the whole 'rest of your life, best of your life' spiel."

CHAPTER EIGHT

Smoke and Mirrors

Olde Pink House

Over the next week, the widows settled into their new lives in Savannah Valley, exercising in the morning, meeting at the pool for a swim, and having lunch together at one of the Tower's lower-level restaurants. They could also be found taking part in the Activity of the Day or visiting each other's homes, followed by dinner at Sky. They made a habit of requesting William's section, much to his delight. Whether said delight was because of the present company or the sizable tips remained to be seen, but no matter, for the widows, interacting with William was near the top of the list of Savannah Valley's most enjoyable amenities.

By the one-month anniversary of the welcome celebration dinner, the Activity of the Day repeated itself, with afternoon card games going on three days running. When it turned up on the schedule for the fourth day in a row, the widows hired a car service to take a day trip to downtown Savannah and have lunch at the Olde Pink House. Glenda called ahead to make reservations, and when informed no tables were available, she booked one of their private dining rooms instead.

It was narrow, with barely enough space to accommodate the twelve-foot-long table, but its baby blue painted walls and white ceiling made it feel much wider. While waiting for their crab cakes with fried green tomatoes to arrive, they polished off their first pitcher of Pink Lady, the house special consisting of freshly squeezed pink lemonade and Absolut Raspberri vodka. They were discussing where to begin their downtown adventure when Darcy let out a heavy sigh.

"Ladies, you know I'm a positive sort of gal, and I don't want to be a total downer, but I can't stop thinking about the fact that the Activity of the Day was afternoon card games *again* today. I'm seriously considering calling Tyler to complain."

Glenda shook her head. "Don't bother. I've left him two messages about that and four more about the golf situation."

Nodding, Edith drained the remnants of her glass. "Agreed. I've left several for both Tyler and Devan and haven't gotten a response. It's ridiculous that we can't get a tee time sooner than a week out. I'm not paying thirty-thousand dollars a month in community dues to wait in line to play one round of golf, and I sure as heck don't want to play card games every single day either. High-stakes poker, maybe, but bridge and canasta? Just saying those names out loud bores me to death."

Sharon snorted. "I don't even know how to play either of those. I mean, I've never played golf before, but at least

with that, I'll get to swing metal rods at balls. Of course, I'll probably miss, but it's the thought that counts, you know?"

The ladies were still laughing when their server arrived with their meals and a fresh pitcher of Pink Lady several minutes later. The crab cakes were delectable, and a comfortable silence descended upon the room. Conversation resumed while they waited for the check and continued planning out the rest of the day. No one had thought to look over the weather forecast before leaving Savannah Valley. When they discovered the forecasted high temperature was ninety-seven degrees, the first order of business became finding a shop that sold hats.

The Mad Hatter was a five-minute walk away, and it being right near the riverfront made it the most attractive option. They emerged a half-hour later with matching wide brim slanted straw hats, each with a different colored silk band. As they continued down River Street toward Peaches and Creme to partake in dessert, which they'd skipped at the Olde Pink House, Darcy stopped in front of the office of Savannah Riverboat Cruises.

"Well, would you look at that? I know we're going on a carriage tour after we have dessert, but—" Darcy pointed at a red and white four-level riverboat docked across the street. "I have always, *always* wanted to hitch a ride on a riverboat queen, as the Creedence fellas said back in the day. Of course, now I can afford to *pay* for a ride."

"Oh please, Darcy. Now you can afford to buy the whole boat." Edith, smirking as she led the way to the offices and held the door open for her friends. "Sounds like a quintessential touristy thing to do. Let's see if they have any openings left for today."

Other than those that conflicted with the carriage tour, no daytime spots were available, so they booked a moonlight top-deck cruise that left the dock at 6:00 p.m. Peaches and Creme was right next door, and the ladies each ordered the house specialty—homemade peach ice cream, served in a cup with a dollop of fresh cream on top. They sat at an outdoor table, enjoying the sounds of the city and the view of the river.

Glenda leaned back in her seat, arms crossed, smiling.

"This is certainly far better than playing any card game there is. My quest to find the most exclusive community to retire to was paramount over the location. But sitting here now, I can have a new appreciation for the draw of Savannah itself. It's like stepping back in time and seeing the world through the eyes of those who've gone before. And we haven't even been on our history tour yet."

Sharon pulled her phone from the pocket of her khaki cargo shorts. "Speaking of which, we've got fifteen minutes until the tour starts." She paused, typing, then scrolled. "We can go back the way we came and turn right on East Bay Street, or we can keep going up River Street, then turn left on Barnard Street, and left again onto West Bay Street. Option one is about four minutes; option two is six."

Edith rolled her eyes, playfully mocking Sharon. "You kids and your darn phones."

Sharon pursed her lips. "Mm-hmm. From what I've seen, you spend twice as much time on yours as I do on mine, lady."

"Listen, Sharon, how else do you expect me to find husband number five? Savannah Valley isn't exactly teeming with eligible bachelors. We have Tyler and Devan, who I might take a free drink from, but other than that, hard pass. The pharmacist is cute, but I saw him holding hands with one of the fitness instructors last week. Normally, that wouldn't knock him out of the running, but the instructor was a guy, and I can't compete with that. Then there's William." Edith fanned herself with her hand, then frowned. "But despite my continued hardcore flirting efforts, it appears he's just not that into me. And I'm reasonably certain as to why."

Darcy leaned forward, elbows on the table. "Share with the class, please, Edith."

Glenda nodded. "Yes, Edith. Do tell."

Edith pointed at Sharon. "I think *she's* the reason why."

Sharon's face scrunched up in disbelief. "Me? Are you serious?"

"Yes, I'm serious. Haven't you noticed the way he looks at you? And whenever we're leaving, it's like he wants to say something after 'goodnight' but doesn't know where to start, so he says nothing *but* 'goodnight.' Maybe he just wants to talk, I don't know, but that look, it's clear he's *interested* somehow. And I don't mean somehow in a 'who could possibly be interested in Sharon' way because you're beautiful and you have a great figure. So, who *wouldn't* be interested?"

Sharon dropped her head in her hands; her voice muffled when she spoke. "Oh my God, I'm going to die of embarrassment right here in front of the remnants of my peach ice cream." She put her hands down, face red and eyes wide. "For clarity, no, I hadn't noticed, but now it will be all I think about whenever I look at him. And with the way my brain works, I'll only be able to last for a short time before I require confirmation of said interest. That's mainly so I can explain that while I think he's a lovely human being, I have no desire to pursue anything other than friendships with my fellow human beings. And that's that. God. I mean, he must be twenty years younger than me. Or more. Ugh. Edith, keep flirting. He'll come around. You have a great figure, too, you know." She stood up. "We need to get moving. And talking about something else, please."

Glenda stood as well. "We can talk about the ladies I

overheard on my walk this morning who were arguing over Eddie Conklin, who lives two doors down from me. His wife Rose passed on two weeks ago, and these gals have been all over him since, stopping by to check in, bringing him meals, and they just discovered that *both* of them were doing the same thing, so they were each demanding the other cease and desist. He's attractive, distinguished, fit, still has all his hair, kind of a Sean Connery air about him, but lord, too soon. Too soon! I'm biding my time before I make my move."

Edith rose, lifting her right hand in the air. "Slap me five, sister."

Chuckling, Glenda did as Edith requested. Darcy got up as well, and they headed off to their destination.

The guide for their private tour was waiting for them, and introduced himself as Jerry and his horse as Beauford. For the next hour and a half, they listened as Jerry eloquently narrated the history of various landmarks and historic homes. When they reached the birthplace of Juliette Gordon Low, founder of the Girl Scouts of the USA, the ladies asked him to stop the carriage so they could walk the grounds and take photos.

When they returned, Jerry offered to take a group photo for them using Sharon's phone. She scrolled through the shots, then emailed them to the others as they reached the end of the tour. It was 5:15, and they took a stroll down the rest of West Bay Street, stopping briefly at Oglethorpe's Bench. It was the spot where the founder of Savannah, General James Edward Oglethorpe, was said to have pitched a tent and spent his first night in Georgia.

As they reached the dock, Darcy shrieked with delight when she noticed that the name of the boat was the Savannah River Queen, then began singing "Proud Mary" a bit too loudly. Edith and Glenda joined in, followed midsong by Sharon, whose passion for music was unparalleled but talent sorely lacking. They found a table for four near the rear of the boat, and dusk had just fallen when the captain launched at 7:00 p.m. As they intended to eat dinner at Sky when they returned to Savannah Valley, in lieu of a full meal, they shared a charcuterie board and a bottle of white wine. As dark descended, the city lights transformed the landscape, and Glenda felt inspired to voice her thoughts on what meaning the day had brought for her.

"While observing the reflections of the light upon the water, I can't help but do a little reflecting of my own. Today, taking our tour and now viewing the city from this vantage point has given me pause. I've seen so many examples of the marks others have left on this world because of their actions. And besides having children, I can't come up with any instances of my having done the same. I'm inspired to rectify that somehow: to exact positive, lasting change." She beamed and shook her head. "Perhaps that's the wine talking."

Darcy reached out and placed her hand over Glenda's. "No, it's not the wine talking. It's my friend Glenda talking. She's at a point in her life where she has the means and ability to make her mark in any way, shape, or form that she sees fit. And I feel blessed to be on this journey with her."

Edith sniffled. "Darn it, Darcy, you need to *stop* with whatever that is. I've cried more since I've known you than I have in the past decade. It's embarrassing."

Sharon leaned over and patted Edith on the back. "Strong women also cry, Edith. Strong women also cry."

"Oh my God, that's from *The Big Lebowski*." Edith's tears turned to laughter. "Sharon, I *love* that movie. You're the *best*."

"Yeah, I know. We should watch it together sometime." Sharon turned to Darcy and Glenda. "Have either of you seen it?" They shook their heads. "Okay. Next Saturday. My place. *Big Lebowski* night. Jeff Bridges at his finest."

Darcy clapped. "Oh, I love me some Jeff Bridges."

Glenda nodded. "I second that sentiment."

Sharon grinned. "Excellent. It's a date, then."

The Savannah River Queen returned to the dock, and when they disembarked ten minutes later, their car was waiting for them. The twenty-minute ride back to Savannah Valley was full of talk of favorite movies, as well as what to have for dinner when they got to Sky.

CHAPTER NINE

As the ladies entered the Tower at 9:30, they noticed a small crowd of residents gathered in the foyer. They could hear brief snippets of the group's conversation as they approached, mainly mentions of "It's closed," and "They're all closed," and "What is going on?" Edith, ever the seeker of information, strode toward the group of residents.

"Wow, what is going on? I was away for the day. Can someone fill me in, please?" She stood, arms crossed, waiting for a response. Darcy, Glenda, and Sharon fell into place behind her. A short gentleman with slicked-back hair wearing blue corduroy pants patterned with tiny golf clubs pointed his cigar in her direction.

"What's going on is they closed the restaurants early. And they're going to close early *every* night from now on."

The blond woman on his arm shook her head. "At 9:00 p.m. Can you believe it? For 'health reasons.'"

Just as she was about to ask for additional details, Edith spotted a sign on the door of the nearest eatery, Sun. She walked over with Darcy, Glenda, and Sharon close behind, and the other residents in tow. She read the words aloud.

"Early to bed and early to rise means keeping yourself healthy. We want to ensure that all our residents live their best lives. So, as part of our Keep Savannah Valley Healthy initiative, our restaurants will now close at 9:00 p.m. But no worries, you can still order from our new *Good Food, Great You* menu until midnight." Edith turned to face the crowd. "What the funky chicken is up with *this*?"

Sharon handed Edith her phone. "Here's the menu. It's all fruit, veggies, low-sodium, low-fat, and whole-grain stuff with baked fish and chicken as meat choices—and *Ensure protein shakes.* Is that word on the sign supposed to be clever?"

Glenda stepped forward and snatched Sharon's phone from Edith. After scanning for herself, her jaw dropped, then closed, clenching tightly. She remained silent for several moments, struggling to rein in her emotions. "While I applaud any effort made to provide us with easy access to healthy food options, I don't believe they should be the *only* options offered. And I simply cannot support management limiting our opportunities to dine out as a way to remind us we need to make sure we get enough rest."

She looked at her friends who were nodding for her to continue. "We're all adults here, fully capable of making our own lifestyle choices and dealing with any repercussions that may arise because of those choices. I'm deeply

disappointed by this recent development. I came to Savannah Valley, at least in part, to avoid this very sort of thing. I resent being viewed as incapable of making my own decisions and treated like a child because I've reached a certain age. The time may come when I am, in fact, incapable, but that's what Savannah Valley Sunset is for, isn't it? I think it's important to discuss this with management right away, but Devan and Tyler haven't responded to my phone calls. Does anyone know where I can find either of them at this hour?"

The crowd was silent, and Sharon removed her phone from Glenda's grasp and typed. She raised her eyes from the screen. "The top two floors of Savannah Valley Sunset are reserved for staff housing. Devan and Tyler have an apartment on the top floor, right across from each other. How convenient."

Glenda turned to everyone and stated that she planned to head over to Sunset right now and asked if anyone would like to join her. Some shook their heads while others glanced at the floor. However, the short cigar guy stepped forward and expressed his thanks for her being willing to speak on their behalf. His blond companion echoed his sentiment, then most of the others. Glenda nodded, then turned on her heel and headed for the front door of the Tower, with Darcy, Sharon, and Edith following.

The Sunset building was a quarter mile up the road,

and it was abundantly clear that Glenda was prepared to march the entire way. Edith took a more practical approach and snagged a golf cart from its charging station in the parking lot. Darcy and Sharon hopped in the back seat, and Edith honked the horn as they pulled up next to Glenda.

"I have now committed 'grand theft golf cart' to support *our* initiative, Locate Savannah Valley Management. Get in, lady. We're a team. The team travels together. Ride or die and all that good stuff."

Glenda stopped for one second before nodding her approval. She smiled as she climbed into the front seat. Edith grinned, put the pedal to the metal, and belted out Springsteen's "Born to Run." When they arrived at Sunset, still chuckling over their impromptu singalong, Edith parked the cart in a full-sized vehicle space. They paused before going inside, discussing how best to address the situation.

Since they'd be representing not just themselves, Glenda felt it was essential to avoid creating any hostility that would cause a division between management and residents, no matter what was tossed at them by the powers that be during their conversation. The ladies agreed they would step in for each other if one of them reached the point where she couldn't continue the discussion in an amicable fashion. As they entered via the main doors, they passed the check-in desk and reached the elevators without encountering a single soul.

Darcy shook her head. “Shouldn’t there be someone at the check-in desk or at least a security guard standing around nearby? Something?”

Glenda grimaced. “Yes. It’s disturbing there’s no one here. Even though they have live-in caregivers, these residents should have an extra layer of protection.” As the elevator doors slid shut, she turned to Sharon. “Do you know which apartments are theirs?”

Sharon grinned. “Of course. P49 and P50. Make a left when we get off. They should be down at the end of the hall.”

“How in the heck did you find that out, Sharon? Man, I wish I knew you when I was still practicing. The problems you could have solved for me.” Edith nodded, the corners of her mouth tilting up in a slight smile.

Sharon tapped her phone screen. “Never underestimate my ability to find things out. That’s my mantra. If it exists on the internet, I’ll find it. If it’s on a device that’s hooked up to the internet, I’ll find it. Though I don’t normally use a phone, it feels pretty good to know I’ve still got it, you know? Plus, this was easy because I went in through the Wi-Fi router, and boom, every computer on the network was wide open, which is so bad. Unsurprising, but bad.”

CHAPTER TEN

Showdown

Glenda stopped and turned to face the door of P50, then rang the bell. No one answered. She rang two more times, then knocked on the door when no one responded. Several minutes passed before they finally heard someone approaching. Edith moved closer to the door just in time to hear a man's voice saying, "Who is that?"

It was followed by another voice, this one closer. "Some old busy-bodies. What do I do?"

Edith stepped back from the door, hands in the air, whispering, "Well, ladies, I'm out already. Sorry. You're amazing, and you've got this."

Before anyone could ask what happened, the door swung inward, and they were treated to a view of Tyler in baggy gray sweatpants and a *Call of Duty* T-shirt, both peppered with what appeared to be Cheetos dust. Devan appeared behind him, clad only in a pair of pineapple-patterned board shorts and neon-green flip-flops, holding an Xbox One controller in his right hand.

Tyler danced around, then started rapping while crossing his arms back and forth in front of him. "So what'cha, what'cha, what'cha want? What'cha want?" He grinned, speaking. “That’s the Beastie Boys. So’s this.” He began again, this time at full volume. “Heeeyyyy laaaaa-diiieesss—get funky. All the ladies in the house, the ladies, the ladies.”

Devan set his controller down on the side table, then grabbed a sweatshirt from the coat rack next to it and quickly pulled it over his head. As he nudged Tyler out of the way, his eyes met Edith’s, and she couldn’t quite discern if what she saw in them was rage or panic—neither of which he’d be able to express if he wished to remain professional.

Though she was enjoying his distress after having heard herself and her friends referred to as old busy-bod-ies, she maintained a neutral expression as he spoke.

“Ladies, please accept my sincerest apologies for Tyler’s behavior. I’m afraid he’s had a bit too much to drink this evening and is not quite himself. But we’ve all been guilty of overindulging a little on our downtime, am I right?” Devan’s tight smile and gritted teeth were evidence of how much it pained him to be polite. “How can I assist you this evening?”

Glenda smiled. “Thank you, Devan. And you’re correct; we’ve all overindulged at one point or another. All part of the human condition. Please accept my apology for our turning up at your residence, but we have had no luck connecting with you via other methods over the past few days.”

Devan clasped his hands together in front of his chest. "Right. Yes, sorry about that. We've been having some major problems with the internal phone systems forwarding to our cells. It seems to be fixed now, but we have a lot of catching up to do, and it's taking some time since we've been hyperfocused on launching the Keep Savannah Valley Healthy Initiative. Have you heard about it yet? It's great, right?"

Glenda nodded. "In fact, that's why we're here. We learned of it when we arrived at the Tower a short while ago for a late dinner at Sky and discovered that all the restaurants were closed. While I fully support and appreciate the offering of healthy meal options, I must admit that I have some concerns about the limitations of the after-hours menu."

Devan smiled as he held up his right hand, palm forward. "Please excuse me for interrupting you, but Brad has requested that we refer questions or concerns about Savannah Valley policies to him so he can address them personally. He feels it's vital that each and every resident knows their voice is important and that he's always ready, willing, and eager to listen to whatever they have to say." He picked up a phone from the side table, tapped, scrolled, then looked back up at the ladies, grinning. "Would you like to schedule a meeting? He's free tomorrow at 3:30."

Glenda gave him a quizzical look. Devan's story made

sense logically, but something didn't ring true. No one had seen Brad on the property since the welcome celebration. The women exchanged knowing glances. The implementation of the new policy blindsided them with no warning. This seemed like a significant overreach of managerial authority.

Glenda turned to her friends.

"Ladies, does that time work for you?" They nodded in agreement, and she turned back to Devan. "Well then, yes, please mark us down for tomorrow at 3:30, and I thank you for taking the time to speak with us. Please enjoy the rest of your evening."

His face lit up with another toothy grin. "Oh, no. Thank *you* for coming. We're always here to help in any way we can. You all have a great night." As he closed the door, Tyler waved at them. They heard the deadbolt click, then the sound of Devan's flip-flops thwacking as the men walked away.

CHAPTER ELEVEN

The Seeds of Rebellion

They sowed the seeds of rebellion during lunch on a Thursday. After a late night of compiling a comprehensive list of questions and suggestions to present during their meeting with Brad, they skipped their usual morning exercise routines and opted for an extended swimming session instead, followed by lunch. Sea was on the bottom floor of the Tower, next to the pool complex, and they were all craving the sea salt and caramel ice cream sundae pie that was a house exclusive. The hostess seated them in a window booth and took their drink orders, and as she walked away, it surprised them to hear a familiar voice.

"Good afternoon, ladies. Fancy meeting you here." William was wearing khaki shorts and a snug forest green polo shirt paired with brown deck shoes. Edith leaned forward to get a better view of his legs.

She grinned as she met his gaze.

"William. So, *this* is what you look like in the light of day. Thumbs up from me."

He laughed. "It serves as evidence that I am not, in fact, a vampire."

Edith was just about to comment further when Darcy nudged her under the table. "Edith, behave yourself; if such a thing is even possible." Edith pressed her fingers to her lips as Darcy continued. "William, honey, you don't usually work down here, do you? I hope this doesn't mean we won't see you at Sky any longer."

"I'm pleased to report that you'll see me both here and at Sky from now on." He smiled as he flipped the page on his order pad. "So, what can I do you for this afternoon? We've got veggie burgers on special, and also on the menu are tilapia fish tacos with lettuce, tomato, corn, and mango salsa, and finally, honey-garlic grilled shrimp served on a bed of brown rice with broccoli on the side." He frowned, scanning his pad for more options, but shrugged his shoulders instead. "We're changing things up a bit here with our offerings—all part of the Keep Savannah Healthy Initiative."

The ladies exchanged looks but refrained from commenting to not upset William, who appeared to be uncomfortable in their presence for the first time since they met him. They all ordered the honey-garlic shrimp, murmuring how delicious it sounded and how much they were looking forward to giving it a try.

As soon as he was out of sight, Darcy shook her head and spoke.

"Gosh, I sure hope William's okay. It seems like

he might have something on his mind. That boy *never* frowns."

The hostess took longer than usual to return with their drinks, and Edith noticed she seemed stressed as well, so much so that it appeared as if she might burst into tears at any moment. Edith asked her name while pressing a hundred-dollar bill into her hand, told her she was doing a great job and that they appreciated her taking such good care of them. The girl smiled, said her name was Samantha, and told Edith that hearing such a nice thing meant the world to her, especially on such a crazy day.

***

Nearly forty minutes passed since they'd ordered, and still no food. Just as Glenda was about to take the last sip of her Bloody Mary, her phone rang. She pulled the device from her purse, brows lifting in surprise at the name that appeared on the screen. "It's Devan. I'm going to put him on speaker." She swiped to answer, then clicked the speaker icon. "Hello, Devan. Please pardon the background noise. We're having lunch at Sea."

"Hi, Mrs. Edleman. Please excuse me for interrupting your meal, but I wanted to make sure I caught you in time. Unfortunately, Brad needs to cancel this afternoon's meeting. He was called away on urgent business overseas and won't be back for a couple of weeks, maybe longer. He said he's sorry for the inconvenience and that while he'd prefer to address your concerns straightaway, we'll just have to put a pin in it for now and circle back to it when he returns from his trip."

He rushed on before anyone could speak. "I'd like to apologize for not being able to resolve this on my own. We all appreciate your patience. Anyway, Sea's great, right? Brand-new menu too. I hope you enjoy. Feel free to reach out if anything else comes up, okay? I'll do my best to help."

The four women shook their heads in tacit agreement they wouldn't respond. Glenda thanked him, then ended the call. She shook her head. "Well, that's discouraging. I'm not sure what to think of all this, honestly. But I'm feeling that Brad may not be as open to hearing our concerns as Devan claims him to be, nor would he take them seriously if he did hear them. If that's true, it's not acceptable. The residents of Savannah Valley deserve better. Anyone who resides in this community deserves better. At the very least, our monthly dues payment should grant us a say in what goes on here. Our voices should be heard."

Darcy nodded. "Absolutely, they should. Loud and clear. We spent so much time last night getting organized, so we'd be able to lay everything out in an easily digestible format for him, and poof, not going to happen. We even trimmed our comments so we wouldn't take up too much of his time, but still get our points across. It's great for an owner to want to handle things personally, but my word!"

Sharon interrupted her. "Sometimes it's not possible, and you need to delegate to the people you hired to manage your property. I mean, the issues we're experiencing right now are important, and while we don't want to *wait* for a resolution, I supposed we *could* wait for one. It's not a life-or-death situation." She took a sip of water before adding, "But what if it was? What happens here if there's a genuine emergency and we need management to act? Last night, we all saw that there's no security at Sunset, and now this. Well, I'm not going to lie. I'm feeling some serious concern regarding resident safety. For real, ladies."

Edith nodded. "I agree. And I just don't get it. As in, it doesn't seem like there's any reason for it. Anyway. I think the next step is—" she paused as William returned with their lunch.

He apologized profusely as he set their plates before them.

"I'm so very sorry it's taken me so long to get these to you." He stood at the edge of their table, eyes cast downward before looking at each of the ladies in turn.

Sharon held his gaze, smiling while waving her hand in a dismissive gesture. "Please, don't give it another thought. It's fine. We're fine." She paused, inspecting the food on her plate before addressing him again. "Short-staffed? I remember how that goes."

He nodded, grabbed a water pitcher to refill their glasses, then turned to go. "Is there anything else I can get you right now?"

He glanced around the room and nodded to a table, waving to get his attention.

Edith's brow furrowed, concern evident in her expression.

"William, is anyone else working the floor with you besides Samantha?"

He grimaced, then shook his head again. In a soft, contrite voice, he answered, "No."

Glenda gasped. "Hold on now. Are you saying it's just you and Samantha here, and you're responsible for all these guests?" He nodded again. She slid to the edge of the booth, then stood. "Well, that just won't do. How can we help, William?"

Sharon, Darcy, and Edith exited the booth as well. Sharon grinned at William. "I'm up for serving. Just tell me where you need me."

Glenda raised her hand. "I'll take orders and clear."

Edith put her hand on her hip, shifting her weight to one side. "Former cocktail waitress, ready, willing, and able to rock this with Samantha."

Darcy pointed her index finger toward the door at the

back of the dining room. "Any chance they need help in the kitchen? I think I'd be of better use there."

William held up both of his hands, palms out. "Ladies, I very much appreciate your offer, but please, you don't have to do this."

Glenda reached out and patted his shoulder. "We know we don't have to, but we *want* to. We'll meet new people. Learn new things. It'll be fun." She turned to her friends. "Right, ladies?"

They nodded in agreement, then got down to business. Two hours later, the lunch rush was over, and the tables cleared just in time for the dinner crew to arrive. This time there were four on shift instead of two. Samantha thanked Edith for all her help and said she would try to squeeze in a shower before heading up to Sky. William expressed his gratitude as well. Sharon asked him if he was pulling a double shift also because of Savannah Valley being short-staffed. He nodded but did not comment.

The women used the ladies' room in the main lobby to freshen up. Sharon shared her experience from working double shifts and reminded them it was both physically and mentally exhausting. "Sometimes it can't be helped when an establishment is on the small side, but a place like Savannah Valley should have plenty of funds to hire enough staff to prevent this from happening.

Glenda chimed in. "I'm starting a list of all the things

that need to be addressed around here. Can you imagine how hard this must be on the staff? They might have to wait weeks for relief."

***

They left Sea, feeling invigorated by being able to help but still a bit tired. As a group, they decided to wait until the following day to determine how to proceed. They agreed that safety and staffing issues were top priorities, and Devan and Tyler needed to find a way for them to speak to Brad sooner instead of later.

An hour after arriving home, Sharon was too annoyed to think rationally, so she flopped on the couch and put on the *Great British Baking Show*, a surefire way to mellow her mood. After four episodes, she took a break and started her list. It overwhelmed her with a craving for something sweet, so she went to the kitchen to investigate her options. Before she could decide on a snack, the doorbell rang.

Sharon never had unexpected guests, and the widows always called or texted each other before dropping by. She shook her head at the thought of labeling them "the widows," when in fact, they were her friends—the closest female friends she ever had. She silently thanked Roger for being the catalyst for such an unexpected, magnificent gift when the doorbell rang again, startling her out of her reverie. She half-jogged to the front door to look at the camera and see who was disturbing her peace. It was William, standing with his hands in the pockets of his jeans, shifting from one boot-clad foot to the other. She froze as she recalled Edith's comments about his interest in her.

She gave herself a pep talk before she opened the door. *Sharon, you can handle this. Don't freak out. Be kind. Let him down easy. You're both adults. You've been an adult way longer, nevertheless, you're both adults.* She gave a quick nod and an affirmation. *Yes. I can do this. I am woman. Hear me roar. Or something like that.*

She turned the deadbolt and opened the door, smiling despite feeling like she might throw up. He spoke first, removing his hand from his pocket and running it through his hair.

"Hello, Sharon. Sorry for disturbing you. It's just, well, I've been meaning to say something since I first saw you. But, anyway, now I'm afraid I won't ever have the opportunity to do so again. And I'll never forgive myself if I don't tell you how much—" he rocked back and forth as though losing his nerve to finish.

Sharon held her breath, wishing she pretended she wasn't home, already rehearsing in her head what she'd say in response.

"—how much *Epigraph* means to me."

She released her breath in a quiet whoosh. *Epigraph*

was a video game series she'd created with Roger. The storyline centered on time travel agents from 2099 who journeyed back to find numbered messages from an unknown entity carved into surfaces of buildings and objects throughout human history. When combined, the messages created a document that provided instructions to build a device that would reverse the effects of climate change. It was the one game she still received royalty checks for, and out of all the work she'd done, it was the thing that she was most proud of. She considered everything he'd said and was about to say thank you when she noticed he was wearing a backpack and two suitcases were resting next to him on her stoop. When she lifted her gaze to look at him, there were tears in his eyes.

He held up his hand, palm toward her.

"I'm sorry. I don't know what I was thinking. You don't even know me and, it's just that, well, they let me go, and I just—"

She cut him off, realizing he probably just lost his livelihood because of what she and her friends did at Sea. A fresh bout of anger rose within her. She waved him inside. "William, no worries. Please. Come in. Let's talk. Bring your stuff, okay?"

He placed his luggage and backpack in the foyer, then followed her into the living room. Sharon sat on the

couch, then patted the cushion next to her. He sat beside her, twisting his fingers. Neither spoke for several minutes until Sharon broke the silence.

"If you don't mind, after you tell me about *Epigraph*, I'd like to reach out to Darcy, Edith, and Glenda and see if they're able to join us. Right now, I'm inclined to hop in my Cybertruck, drive it through the Tower doors and light everything on fire, so I think I could use some additional input."

William chuckled. "No, I don't mind at all, and I appreciate you allowing me to speak with you privately first." He closed his eyes, took a deep breath, then opened them, but avoided eye contact. "That first night, at Sky, when I saw you, I just couldn't believe it. Sharon Wright, sitting at my table. That's the real reason I forgot to take your drink order, by the way. Talk about being caught off-guard. Anyway, about *Epigraph*. That game—the game you and Roger created together—it saved my life." He paused, glancing sideways as though she might burst out laughing because of how ridiculous he sounded. But she said nothing. "I know that sounds ludicrous, but—"

She reached out and patted his arm. "Oh no, it doesn't. I just binge-watched four episodes of a baking show so I wouldn't go ballistic and kill someone. No judgment here. Carry on."

A smile flashed across his face before the frown took over. When their eyes met, he looked away, but she recognized something in them she was all too familiar with—grief. He ran his hand through his hair again, then continued. "Twelve years ago, my wife Lizzie, died during childbirth. Our daughter Melody died too." Sharon took his hand in hers and squeezed gently, encouraging him to continue.

"I wasn't even there when it happened. I was in a business meeting, and cellphones were prohibited because what we were discussing was highly confidential. It was two hours before I found out. I had to tell the hospital what we decided to name the baby so they could get all the proper papers together. It turned out that Lizzie had preeclampsia, but it was our first pregnancy, and we didn't know to look for the signs and symptoms. She'd tried to call me before she dialed emergency services." Quiet tears streamed down his cheeks.

Sharon reached for his other hand and held them both in a warm embrace. "I'm so sorry, William. Take your time."

He nodded and continued. "Thank you. And I'm sorry for your loss as well. I read online about Roger's passing. It's an awful thing to have in common, but it's comforting to talk to someone who understands. After that, I gave away most of our things and put what remained in storage, then left London for New York City. I was twenty-eight, and my life was over, but for some reason, I was still breathing. I made ends meet with the proceeds from Lizzie's life insurance policy. And then one day, another dark day in a string of what seemed like endless dark days, I was watching gaming playthroughs on YouTube, so I wouldn't step in front of a bus and end it all. Then I stumbled upon *Epigraph*."

"You did?" she asked, surprise in her voice.

He nodded. "I bought a copy on eBay and got completely, utterly lost in it. It gave me a reason to get up in the morning. It gave me a reason to keep going. It got me through. I started waiting tables, discovered that I enjoyed it immensely, and made a career of it. I know I'm not making any sense. But to think it was that choice that led me to encounter its creator is bonkers. I just wanted to thank you, Sharon, and Roger, for your genius and creativity. The world you built together changed mine for the better, and I will be forever grateful not just for the game, but that you allowed me to share my story with you and express my thanks."

With tears running down her face, Sharon let go of his hands and stood, indicating that he should do the same. She opened her arms wide. "Come on, William. Bring it in. Us widows and widowers must stick together. Especially when one of them may have played a significant role in getting the other *fired*." She paused, staring into his eyes, waiting for confirmation that her assumption was correct.

He stepped forward, nodding, and they embraced, gingerly at first, then with more confidence. William laughed.

Sharon pulled back so she could see his face. "What's funny? Inquiring minds want to know."

He cocked his eyebrows. "Does this mean I can join your club?"

"What club?"

He snorted. "The Rich Widows club. Granted, I'm not rich, and technically not a widow, but—"

She broke their embrace, crossing her arms and tilting her head. "And how would you know about that?"

He tapped an index finger to his right ear. "Your servers are always listening, Sharon. And people tend to forget that we're there, so we get to hear, you know, things. So many, many things."

"Well, *that's* terrifying. Speaking of, I'm going to call my gal pals now." She frowned, her mood shifting as the gravity of his situation hit her. "William, I promise you we're going to make this right, okay? And if it's going to take a little time to make it right, we'll make sure you have everything you need in the interim." He opened his mouth to speak, but she raised her hand to cut him off. "Nope, not a word. Your future is in jeopardy because of us, and it's the least we can do. End of story."

He nodded once, and Sharon grabbed her phone from the coffee table, calling in her reinforcements one by one.

***

While they waited, Sharon asked William if he wanted her to keep what he shared private. He said he didn't mind the others knowing, but he asked her to fill them in when he wasn't present. She knew how he felt all too well. Retelling her own story was like reliving it all over again. Glenda arrived first, followed by Darcy and Edith, who shared a golf cart. They each hugged William in turn, and Edith was the only one who had the presence of mind to ask him the specific reason his employment was terminated. He confirmed it was because of their helping with the lunch service.

Devan said fraternizing with the residents was against company policy listed in the employee handbook. Glenda asked if they ever provided him with a handbook or if he had signed anything showing he agreed to company policies. He said he had not, and Edith told him he likely had grounds for a wrongful termination suit. She asked when he was expecting his next paycheck. William blushed, admitting that he had only received one check since he started and that the staff shortage was due to most deciding to leave after not receiving their paychecks.

William told them Devan and Tyler promised the issue would be resolved by the next pay period. He agreed to stay because he had nowhere to go and no funds to get there anyway. Edith explained that, besides possible wrongful termination, he had a valid claim to sue for wage theft. After more discussion, they agreed it would be best for him to leave Savannah Valley straightaway so he wouldn't be connected to whatever might transpire as the ladies sought a resolution to their issues with the management.

Sharon booked him a suite at the Bohemian downtown while Glenda called a car service to meet him outside the gates of the property. He resisted at first, but the pressure and encouragement from the four women convinced him he had no choice. They agreed he should walk to the gates so he could avoid being seen with any of them and potentially create additional problems. The widows watched from the front window as he made his way from Sharon's driveway and disappeared into the night.

As soon as they were seated in the living room, Glenda pointed at Sharon. "Sharon, I believe you have some explaining to do."

Edith nodded. "Oh yes, she does. I told you he was interested, and yours is the first place he thought to go, did he?"

Sharon held up her hand, stopping Edith from continuing. Her firm tone left no room for argument.

"Stop. It's not what you think at all. He recognized me at the welcome celebration, and he has wanted to talk to me about one of my games ever since, but the opportunity never presented itself. He figured this would be his last chance. William lost his wife and daughter twelve years ago. They both died during his daughter's birth. Playing my game helped him through his grief, and he wanted to thank me." She leaned back on the sofa, her forearm covering her eyes.

Edith moved beside her, leaning in to whisper near her ear. "Sharon, I'm so sorry. Sometimes I take things too far. Please forgive me."

Sharon let her arm fall to her side. "No need to apologize. There's no way anyone could have known any of that. I'm sorry I snapped at you." She shifted gears. "And to express how sorry I am, I will share two additional tidbits of information regarding what occurred before you arrived, aside from both of us crying and recalling brutally unhappy memories. Number one, I hugged him. Number two, he smells amazing." She shrugged, her grin fading. "But it's feeling like something might be very wrong with this place."

Glenda nodded. "Yes, it does. We need to put our heads together and find out *what* that something is."

Edith stood and turned to face the other women. "And I'm pretty sure I know right where to start. Sharon, remember when you said if a device is hooked up to the internet—"

"—I'll find it. Edith, I love your *mind.* When I was poking around last night, I found the building plans and which apartments were Devan's and Tyler's because the network here is wide open. I could sail an ocean liner through the back door they left open. Any computer that's powered on, I can get into. Most offices never shut down fully anymore because no one wants to wait for them to boot in the morning. Wow. Okay. This is happening. Let's adjourn to my war room, ladies. It's time to rock and roll."

Sharon's war room was a spare bedroom filled with all her electronic equipment, including video game systems, laptops, computer towers, and a slew of other items the other ladies had never seen before. A chair that looked like it came from the control deck of the Starship Enterprise rested in front of an array of five monitors, the largest one in the middle, the size of what most folks used as televisions. They watched as she worked, fingers flying across the keyboard with unbelievable speed. Ten minutes later, she threw both hands in the air, then pointed at a side screen.

"Look at that. Not only is Devan's computer *on,* but he has his email and a bunch of other stuff open, including the program they use for accounting, so I don't even need to figure out the logins. My God, this is the easiest hack I've

ever done in my entire life. It's like Halloween, Christmas, and my birthday all rolled into one."

Over the next hour and a half, they read through email chains that included Brad, Tyler, and Devan that dated as far back as the day after the welcome celebration. In many instances, they'd referred to residents as "sheep," "brain-damaged," the "walking dead," and most notably, "cash cows." A week after the welcome celebration, an email with the subject of "Let's Roll" sent by Brad advised Tyler and Devan that everything was "set" and they could start "allocating revenue" to the new account. Sharon turned to Edith, who was reading from over her shoulder along with Darcy and Glenda.

"I detect the scent of, oh, I don't know, embezzlement, maybe? Tell me, my wise attorney friend. Do you smell it too?"

Edith nodded. "I do indeed. Pull up that accounting program for me and let me sit, will you? Remember the date of that email, please."

Sharon snorted, dragged the browser window displaying Devan's email account to another monitor, opened the accounting program on the main screen, then vacated her spot.

Edith took her place, sticking her tongue out as she sat down. "Show off. Okay, let's have a look-see, shall we?" She examined the chart of accounts, then opened one register. Then another. Then another. Fifteen minutes later, she leaned back in the chair, pressing her fingers to her temples. "Holy—! Holy—! Help me. I can't even find the right string of expletives to use. This is so much worse than I could have ever imagined. I figured they were maybe skimming a few extra thousand, maybe a hundred thousand each, but there are no words to describe this."

"I've got a few choice words, but I'll keep them to myself," Glenda's outrage was palpable.

Edith continued. "And here we thought they didn't care about Savannah Valley's residents. Instead, good lord, they're *criminals*. That's why they were cutting back on stuff, to keep the con going as long as possible. Ladies, they've taken everything. Everything. And what they didn't *spend*, they transferred to offshore accounts."

"What?" the chorus of voices filled the room.

Edith pointed to the screen. "And, on top of *that*, they've accumulated a veritable mountain of debt. So much so that our combined dues aren't enough to pay the bills each month. I can't believe I'm saying this, but Savannah Valley is *bankrupt*."

Sharon and Darcy stood, stunned, with mouths agape. But Glenda smiled, stepping forward to put her hands on Edith's shoulders. "Edith, you say that like it's a bad thing."

Edith rose from the chair, eyes wide. "It is a bad thing. A very, very bad thing. A very, very *big* bad thing. Right

Sharon? Right, Darcy?" Darcy nodded, but Sharon's brow furrowed as the right side of her mouth curled upward in a lopsided grin.

"Glenda, I do believe I see where you're going with this. And I like it. I like it a *lot*."

Edith blinked her eyes. "I don't get it. What could make this an un-bad thing? There's no money. We'll be lucky if we get a third of what we paid for our houses."

Glenda raised her right index finger. "Ah, Edith, but there *is* money."

Darcy's eyes lit up. "*Our* money."

Glenda nodded. "Yes. Our money. This is it, ladies. This is our opportunity to make our mark on the world. It starts here, in Savannah Valley. We can transform this place into what we expected it to be, and then some. We will turn it into a community designed not for people to grow old but for them to just grow and keep growing—together. You all in?"

They piled their hands atop each other's, shouted 'Yes!' in unison, then set about the business of bringing down the house of cards Brad, Devan, and Tyler had built.

CHAPTER TWELVE

New Dawn, New Day

Three weeks later, the Rich Widows stood in the same spot where Brad, Tyler, and Devan had stood during the welcome celebration as they waited for the residents of Savannah Valley to finish filtering in. Everyone knew about the scandal, as the Feds had come in the dark of night three days after the ladies alerted them to apprehend Tyler and Devan. They confiscated their computers and a varied assortment of electronic devices and carton upon carton of paperwork. Brad was discovered, not overseas, but hiding off the coast of the Florida Keys on the yacht he purchased with stolen funds. All three men were being held without bail and would not see the outside world again for quite some time.

Since the raid, the restaurants were closed, along with the golf course, pool, and gym. Some residents had cut their losses and vacated Savannah Valley but agreed to come back for this meeting, which had been presented to them as an exit seminar. Rumors circulated, and the ladies did not intervene lest they surrender the element of surprise. Once the tables were full, Glenda stepped up to the podium and spoke into the microphone.

“Hello there, my fellow Savannah Valley residents. I’d like to start by apologizing for summoning you here under false pretenses. This is not, in fact, an exit seminar.” She gave a moment for the expected whispering and mumbling. Then, in a louder voice, she continued, “At least, I hope it isn’t. I know these past few weeks have been challenging for us—in many ways, they’ve been devastating. I’ve felt that myself. Our futures here, our futures in general, are no longer clear.”

The heads in the room nodded in unison.

Glenda took a sip of water from the glass on the podium and continued. “That’s difficult to bear at any age, but for us, thinking we were settled and faced only smooth sailing until the end of the line—well, I don’t have to tell you, it’s even more difficult. Today, you’re here because I have news to share with you. Important news regarding the future of our community. Good news, as far as I’m concerned.”

The room was silent, all eyes on Glenda. “I’m here to announce that Savannah Valley has a buyer. We are back in business. We signed the paperwork an hour ago. I’d like you to meet the new owner—or rather, owners.”

Staff circulated with glasses of champagne, and the residents turned their heads from side to side, looking around, expecting the new owners to appear. Glenda waited until everyone had a glass of bubbly, then waved

Darcy, Edith, and Sharon to the podium to join her. "It's us. We're the new owners—the Rich Widows of Savannah Valley. And we have big plans to make even bigger changes. Positive changes. Amazing changes. Because you deserve nothing less than, well, *everything*. We hope with all our hearts that you'll stick around. Because as far as we're concerned, this is, to paraphrase *Feelin' Good*, a new dawn, a new day, a new life—for you, for me, for all of us. Sharing the best of our lives—together!" She raised her glass to the room. "To Savannah Valley."

Every single person in the room stood and cheered—including William, who they convinced to come back to take on the position of executive director. He raised his glass to the toast.

The toast was goodbye to what Savannah Valley was and a celebration for all that Savannah Valley was going to be.

EPILOGUE

Glenda, Sharon, Darcy, and Edith are just getting started! They've proved that they can work together and do good things.

But now they're ready to take on bigger issues! The four widows on their way to learning that as seniors, they are still in the game, and they can still have fun and still make a difference. But this time they're after bigger game.

What are the issues you care about? As I start the next book in the Rich Widows series, tell me the issues that you wish the Widows would take on? Since my issue is human trafficking, that's almost certainly going to be one of them.

But maybe it's an issue to deal with in a later book. I'm open as can be for suggestions where we combine adventure and having a meaningful life, and maybe leaving a legacy of trying to make the world a better place.

Write to me and tell me what you think!

My address is: Mitzi@AuntMitzi.com

If you'll write, two things will happen. First, I promise to answer you. After all, I wrote this book for you, so the least I can do is give you an answer. But second, you can have a serious impact on what issues we get into in future books.

We have to stay in touch, right? I'm looking forward to hearing from you!

Love,
Mitzi

It's Review Time

Please leave a review. It would mean so much to me. I wanted to share this story about real women who never give up. Who do you know needs inspiration on how to not be taken advantage of? To call out wrong things when they see them and then make things right for themselves as well as others around them. The more people know about this book, maybe, they too can come to terms with what's going on in their life, no matter their age.

Good or bad, I want to hear from you. All it takes is one little sentence, more is good too. I just want to know if you enjoyed this book.

https://www.amazon.com/Rich-Widows-Savannah-Valley-Earned-ebook/dp/B0BBXCQ4K2/

ABOUT MITZI PERDUE

Author, speaker, and businesswoman Mitzi Perdue holds a BA with honors from Harvard University and an MPA from the George Washington University. She is a past president of the 35,000-member American Agri-Women, She's also a former syndicated columnist for *Scripps Howard* and her column, "The Environment and You", was the most widely-syndicated environmental column in the country. Her television series, *Country Magazine*, was syndicated to 76 stations. She's the founder of CERES Farms, the second-generation family-owned commercial and agricultural real estate investment company that has owned rice fields, commercial and residential real estate, and today, the family vineyards sell wine grapes to wineries such as Mondavi, Bogle, Folie a Deux, and Toasted Head.

Mitzi combines the experiences of three long-time family businesses. Her father Ernest Henderson co-founded the Sheraton Hotel Chain and her late husband Frank Perdue was the second generation in the poultry company that today operates in more than 100 countries. She herself founded CERES Farms in 1974.

She loves to point out that the Henderson family business began in 1840 with the Henderson Estate Company and they have been having yearly family reunions since 1890. If you combine the 179 years since it began, and the 99 years that Perdue Farms has been in business, and the 45 years since the founding of Ceres Farms she represents more than three centuries of family business history.

Recently she authored *How to Make Your Family Business Last, Techniques, Advice, Checklists, and Resources for Keeping the Family Business in the Family.*

Mitzi Perdue likes nothing better than to share tips for what worked in the long-running families that she's a part of.

www.ingramcontent.com/pod-product-compliance
Lightning Source LLC
Chambersburg PA
CBHW051109030726
47504CB00006B/1868

9798885810012